'Oh, it's you!' E

His smile grew. 'Yes, i
a bouquet of carefully ~~~~~~~ ~~~~~~~ uecause
there wasn't time. But at least offering an apology
for my quick temper this afternoon.'

What game was Lewis playing? He didn't seem
the sort to say sorry for anything he'd done so she
decided he was trying to flirt with her. But, just as
she was about to say something sharp, she realised
that he was quite serious. Then she saw that strange
loneliness come into his eyes again and felt her
heart softening, so she smiled back at him.

'Apology accepted,' she said quietly. 'I was as
much to blame.'

Born in the Midlands, **Jenny Bryant** now lives in Surrey. As she was an only child, books became her best friends, and she began writing stories from the age of eight. After attending drama school she followed a variety of careers, including theatre production and teaching creative writing to adults. Now widowed, she often visits her children and grandchildren who, she says, keep her up to date. She also has a number of doctor cousins happy to advise on medical matters.

A LOVING PARTNERSHIP

BY

JENNY BRYANT

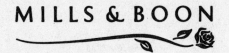

MILLS & BOON

*MILLS & BOON, the Rose Device and
LOVE ON CALL are trademarks of the publisher.
Harlequin Mills & Boon Limited,
Eton House, 18-24 Paradise Road, Richmond, Surrey TW9 1SR*

© Jenny Bryant 1996

ISBN 0 263 79855 0

*Set in Times 10 on 11$\frac{1}{2}$ pt. by
Rowland Phototypesetting Limited
Bury St Edmunds, Suffolk*

03-9610-47218

Made and printed in Great Britain

CHAPTER ONE

DR ERYL THOMAS thought the journey from the Midlands to Wales would never end. The weather was unbearably hot for early June and the Friday traffic exhausting. But, more than that, she found returning here after all this time a traumatic experience. And as she drove into the foothills of Cader Idris, with the grime of the Black Country far behind her, she wondered if she had been wise to accept the post of GP in a place that had once held so much pain.

The mountain, known in English as the Chair of King Idris, hovered like a benign sentinel over many of the villages in this part of mid-Wales. Particularly Dynas, the place where she had been born. A place that she had finally left in despair. When Eryl was still a child her mother had died in the shadow of this mountain and it was here that her father had practised as a GP until he, too, had died.

It was also the place where she had fallen hopelessly in love for the first time, only to suffer grief when that love turned sour.

Could she face up to those old memories? Rid herself of them once and for all so that she would be able to live here again?

She slowed down, easing the car towards the edge of a narrow track, then parked it so that it was half hidden by a boulder. Nothing seemed to have changed. The view was still magnificent. Vast and empty, the only signs of civilisation in this stark Welsh valley were a few remote farmhouses with sheep grazing among rocky outcrops.

Getting out of the car, she stretched and ran her fingers through the pale russet curls of her short hair. Then she slipped off her shoes, loving the soft feel of moss beneath her feet. At last, raising her face to the mountain, she breathed in pure air and savoured the tangy scent of wild thyme mingling with heather.

A sudden gust of wind tugged at her cotton skirt, lifting it until it billowed around her like a soft yellow cloud. Laughing aloud with a sense of freedom, she clutched at it, struggling to tuck her skimpy white blouse inside the waistband. Whatever her new job was like it would be heaven compared with the general practice she'd just left. Surely nothing could be as crucifying as that. Situated on the outskirts of Birmingham, she had found it little better than a factory where patients arrived and then left one after another in quick succession. There had been no time to deal with the person—just the sick body.

As far as Eryl was concerned this was definitely not what medicine was all about. So, when the chance had come to leave she'd taken it, quite sure that work in Dynas would be different. Even if the village had changed since she'd last seen it, at least it would still have some soul.

When she'd spotted the announcement in a medical journal inviting applications for the post of an extra GP in Dynas—which it described as a fast-growing rural area—her first reaction had been to ignore it. But, after tussling with doubts, she had applied. Soon afterwards, instead of a written reply, she had received a phone call from Dr Trefor Dillon, the senior partner, suggesting an interview.

'I just happen to be visiting your area soon so we could meet somewhere in Birmingham,' he'd said.

Eryl had been mystified. Surely her letter of application hadn't been so brilliant that it had merited a personal call like that. The moment she'd replaced the receiver she'd sought out her senior partner in the Midland practice, telling him about the interview arrangement and asking if he found it as strange as she did.

Her colleague had shrugged. 'Not particularly. As the man says, he'll be in the area. But even if he was making a special journey it would make sense.'

'What on earth do you mean?'

'Well, you're Welsh and this is a Welsh practice. So what could be more natural?' He'd laughed softly. 'Perhaps your fame has spread and he can't wait to meet you!'

'A likely story!' she'd scoffed, grinning back at him.

The interview had taken place in a Birmingham hotel. It had been informal and pleasant but at the end of it she had been shocked into silence. Not only had she immediately been offered the job—and a flat to go with it—she'd also discovered that Dr Dillon's surgery was the very one where her father had practised medicine.

Had this kindly, white-haired Welshman known? Had he chosen her because he'd once met her father? Perhaps heard of his death and wondered what had happened to the rest of the family?

As Dr Dillon had looked at her, he'd seemed to read her thoughts in some uncanny way for he'd said earnestly, 'It's your work record that impressed me, young lady. Oh, I realise you were born in Dynas. I also know your father was once a GP there. But I never met him so this isn't a case of nepotism.'

He had then given her an impish smile that had also been filled with tremendous warmth. And for one moment she'd regarded him more like an elderly uncle than a senior partner.

Now, standing alone on the mountainside, she remembered that smile and tried to push her doubts aside. All that mattered was facing up to a new life in a place that she would always think of as home, whatever had happened there. Somehow she would eventually find the strength to lay all those old ghosts.

Suddenly she noticed another car hurtling down the hillside towards her. The man she glimpsed at the steering-wheel must be some sort of mad joyrider, she thought resentfully. As he sped towards her car, which he obviously hadn't seen, she slipped on her shoes and moved swiftly to the track, waving furiously at him to make him stop. His tyres squealed, sending up a shower of pebbles as he came to a slithering halt just inches from the nose of her bonnet.

The face glaring at her through the open window was suntanned, the dark brown eyes filled with anger. 'What the devil d'you think you're doing?' he shouted. 'Stepping out like that, you could have got us both killed!'

A Scot, she thought, by the trace of accent. And, by the look of his complexion, some airhead of a playboy with enough leisure to soak up the Mediterranean sun.

'You're a fine one to talk!' she retorted. 'Driving like that, you're the one who's lethal!'

He opened his mouth as if he was going to say something scathing and then changed his mind. 'Move your car, will you? I'm in a hurry.'

'Off to some party or other, I suppose,' she said, her voice withering.

He ignored her. 'Just back up into that space behind you and let me pass!'

The last thing she wanted was a prolonged argument in this heat so she did as he asked. But not before she had made a mental note of his registration number, afterwards scribbling it on an envelope as he swooped past her and drove—just as dangerously as before— down the mountainside and out of sight.

After managing to control her irritation, she eased her way onto the track again, drove over the hills to the other side of the mountain and then on to Dynas.

The moment she saw the place her heart sank. Changed? It was unrecognisable. From a village it had grown into a small town, where holiday caravans sprawled down one hillside and little square bungalows climbed in neat rows up another. There was also a new modern-looking school built near the old church.

After driving through streets with names she did not recognise, she eventually found herself outside the old house where she had been born. It still looked familiar, although the surgery built at one side of it in her father's day now had a large extension.

Wearily, and with a fresh sense of anxiety filling her, she left the car, opened a wrought-iron gate and walked up a flagged path to the front door of the house.

The old-fashioned bell had been replaced by a button that activated a two-way microphone concealed behind grating in a metal box. As she pressed it she wondered why Dr Dillon needed such a safety device in a peaceful place like this.

'Yes? Who is it?' said an impersonal female voice, somewhat distorted by the grating.

'Dr Thomas. From England.'

'Push the door and come in.'

No 'please' or 'thank you', Eryl noted wryly. After she heard a click she did as she was told, shivering slightly as she looked around the imposing hall she remembered so well. Wondering what on earth was going to happen next, she waited for a few moments, suddenly tempted to giggle as she pictured herself in the middle of a horror movie.

At last a door opened on the landing above and a tiny middle-aged woman dressed in black descended the stairs, a frown marring what could have been a pleasant, pink-cheeked face.

'You're early!' she accused.

'Er—yes. I'm sorry. If it's inconvenient I'll go away and come back again later.'

The woman stared at her with hostile eyes, then muttered something in Welsh. Because this was Eryl's first language she understood every word and what she heard riled her.

'I beg your pardon!' she said heatedly, using the native tongue. 'I'll have you know that I am not an ignorant pig of an Englishwoman, as you put it. Even though I've worked in the Midlands. For goodness' sake, I was *born* here! In this very house.'

The woman looked taken aback. Crumpled, somehow. And Eryl began to feel sorry for her. Sorry, too, for her own short-tempered reaction.

A moment later she heard a man chuckle quite near her. Then Dr Dillon emerged from the shadows on the ground floor and said, 'Well done, my dear! It's best to start as you mean to go on! But let me assure you, Mrs Reynolds has a bark that's much worse than her bite.'

*   *   *

Tea and scones, served in Dr Dillon's private sitting-room on the ground floor, were more than welcome, even though they were dished out by the disagreeable Mrs Reynolds, who kept staring at Eryl as if she were a visitor from outer space.

When the woman left, bustling out with an air of wounded self-importance, Trefor Dillon relaxed visibly, giving a little sigh before he smiled at Eryl. 'Sorry about that,' he said. 'I've tried to persuade my house-keeper not to be so brittle. And, believe me, she has improved. But today you must have caught her on the hop, as they say.'

Eryl laughed. 'I think that phrase sounds even better in Welsh, don't you? More telling.' She stayed silent for a moment, then asked, 'Is there any reason why she's so unfriendly?'

'Oh, yes. More than one, I'm afraid. A bad marriage years ago. Multiple deaths in the family. Even trouble with the law when she decided to march with a protest movement. Something to do with Welsh rights, I believe.'

Eryl was astounded. 'And here was I thinking of Dynas as a peaceful place,' she said.

'Has any community ever been truly at peace?'

'I used to think so when I lived here. That is, until I. . .' She stopped in mid-sentence before she could say things that she knew she would regret. She would have to be wary of the kindness in this man's deep blue Celtic eyes, which were now looking into her own green ones as if they were seeking out her very soul.

At last he looked away and murmured, 'Of course you will use your professional discretion over my remarks about Mrs Reynolds, won't you?' Although he spoke firmly his words were tempered by that wonderful smile that immediately warmed her heart. 'She used to be my patient but even though she left to sign on elsewhere, technically freeing me from obligation, I really shouldn't have spoken like that.'

'Of course. I'll be discretion itself!' Eryl assured him.

'Good. Now it's time I put you in the picture about your work here. But, first, I must explain something I didn't mention at your interview.'

'Oh?' Eryl frowned.

'You needn't look so worried, my dear! I just want you to know why I'm creating this extra partnership. Not only is the place growing but I've decided on early retirement. In fact, I'm already cutting down on my own work.'

'You're not well?' Eryl asked anxiously.

He smiled again, suddenly looking like a man of forty instead of someone who was probably sixty plus. 'Never felt better, my dear! But I do like to have some leisure time for golf and fishing, my two main passions since I became a widower twenty years ago.'

She wondered why such an attractive man had never remarried, then remembered what her father had said when her mother had died all those years ago. 'I'll never find another woman to match her,' he'd told her as he'd arranged for his sister to bring up his only child.

'I think you'll fit the bill here perfectly,' Trefor Dillon went on. 'My partner's out on a case at the moment so I'll introduce you when he returns. You're sure to like him.'

Eryl just nodded, saying nothing.

Trefor hesitated for a moment and then said, 'I've invited him for supper tonight after his evening surgery.

At about eight. Will you also do me the honour of dining with me?'

There was such a lovely, old-world charm about this man that she couldn't possibly refuse so she said, 'Thank you. That's kind.' Then, wondering what this anonymous doctor would be like, she asked, 'What's your partner's name?'

'Lewis Caswell. An Englishman Mrs Reynolds has actually learnt to tolerate.' He chuckled. 'It took some time, believe me. But because his mother was a Scot she soon realised that some Celtic blood was better than none!'

Eryl had forgotten the prejudice that had always existed here. Now she suddenly felt as if she had stepped back into ancient history where the English were the perpetual enemy, despite the unity brought about by the first Prince of Wales centuries ago.

Dr Dillon eased himself out of his chair. 'Come! Let me show you around the place before Lewis returns. Shall we start with the surgery we've just set up for you?'

It took some time before she had seen everything. Her father's old surgery had been turned into a treatment room, she noticed. The extension that she'd spotted from the road formed the main part of the practice and was empty now, presumably waiting for evening surgery to begin.

Well furnished, it had a comfortable waiting area, supplied with magazines and children's toys, a reception desk with several telephones and three rooms beyond, acting as separate surgeries. Her own was small but adequate, with an immaculate examination bed, a computer on a large desk with a locked drugs cupboard behind it, a sink with towels and soap and all the other everyday necessities.

'We have two receptionists who come in each day. Glynis Jones and Betty Williams,' he said. 'Surgery is open from nine till twelve with afternoons free for visits and appointments with our two nurses who come in to give injections and so on.'

'They use the treatment room we saw when we first came in?'

'Yes, they do. But it's also used as an isolation area.'

'Really?' Eryl was surprised. 'In what way?'

Trefor chuckled. 'Maybe your patients in the Midlands were more disciplined than ours. Kept their infections away from the surgery and waited for a home visit. But, here, I'm afraid some of our patients regard the practice as a kind of shrine that must be visited regularly. Even bringing in their children suffering from measles and suchlike!'

'I see,' Eryl said slowly. Then she asked, 'Has anything been done to stop this sort of thing?'

'Of course. But re-education is not accepted easily here. People insist that the old ways are best.'

She glanced at him, wondering if she should tell him what had just occurred to her and then came out with it impulsively. 'Would you mind if I tried to deal with this? When I get to know the patients, of course. Perhaps a word or two from someone new might be more acceptable to them.'

Instead of looking offended, he seemed extremely pleased. 'Would you really do that? Perhaps make it your special mission?'

'I'd be glad to. That is, if Dr Caswell doesn't object. I tried to do something similar in Birmingham but I'm afraid it fell through because of pressure of work.'

'A pity. But, never mind, maybe we can make it work in Dynas.' He began to look enthusiastic. 'I'd like to set up a special clinic for you. Leave you to run it how you like.'

He then went on to tell her about her other duties. Evening surgery was at six and the working week from Monday to Friday, with Saturday mornings kept for emergencies only.

A touch of amusement came to his eyes as he said, 'Hopefully, on Sunday we rest. Unless we get called out, of course.'

'What happens about night calls?'

'Naturally we have a roster, sometimes sharing the work with a surgery in Pandy—the village just over the low hills.'

She knew only too well where Pandy was. Knew the surgery, too. That was where Robert had practised medicine. For a moment she was taken back, living again all the heartache of that time. But the moment passed as she deliberately pulled herself into the present.

'I see,' she said. 'Sounds like a very busy life for a small place.'

Trefor gave a low chuckle. 'I hope I haven't put you off. But the advertisement did warn that this place was growing, didn't it?'

'Oh, don't worry. I like nothing better than to be kept busy.'

'I gathered that at your interview. Now, if you're ready, I'll show you the small flat that goes with the job.'

She followed him across a courtyard at the far side of the house to what had once been the old stable block.

'I used to play here as a child,' she said, pleased to

see ample room for parking in the courtyard as there was little space near the surgery extension.

She noticed one car there already and, seeming to read her thoughts with that knack she'd noticed at the interview, he admitted that it was his.

'I hope you won't mind a clutter of cars here during the day,' he said.

'No. Why should I?'

'Because this is virtually your own private courtyard. Only staff members are allowed to park here, of course. And I'm sure they'll respect your privacy.'

She really didn't care whether they did or not. Once she was installed she could surely ward off the too curious.

The place had been improved with tubs of azaleas and hydrangeas, placed attractively on either side of an oak front door with a brass letter-box halfway down.

Inside, the stable was unrecognisable. On the ground floor was a tiny hall, where a telephone rested on an antique table with a wooden chair beside it. Carpeted stairs led to the landing above, where there was a well-furnished bedroom at the back with another telephone on a shelf beside the bed. Nearby was a bathroom with everything a single person would need, including a bath with shower attachment and shelves for toiletries.

At the front of the building was a small but elegantly furnished sitting-room, with casement windows over-looking the courtyard. Next to it was a serviceable kitchen.

'It's perfect!' Eryl exclaimed. 'What a wonderful job you've made of the old place.'

He gave her an impish grin then began to look proud of himself. 'I hope you'll be happy here,' he said.

'I'm sure of it,' she replied, amazed to find that she

really meant it. Then she asked, 'Does Dr Caswell live in the main house?'

'Lewis? No, he doesn't. I offered him rooms when he first came here but he prefers to live away from his work so he rents a small cottage in the village.' Trefor studied her closely for a moment. Then he said, 'He's rather a shy, private kind of person, you see. But, in spite of that, I'm sure you'll work well together.'

They were in the sitting-room when she heard a car driving into the courtyard.

Trefor smiled suddenly and said, 'Here he is now. So come and be introduced. Then later we can all have supper together.'

She peered out of the open casement window and took in a sharp breath.

She would know that car anywhere, she thought. And the registration number, which had been etched indelibly on her mind only an hour or so ago. The man now slamming the driver's door could not be forgotten in a hurry, either.

As he looked up at her, her heart plummeted.

A pair of dark brown eyes were staring straight at her, looking surprised at first and then turning to that swift anger she'd seen on the mountain.

Yet, now, there was also something else. A kind of loneliness in him, which surprised her. She also found it strangely touching. And, quite against her will, she wanted to reach out to him. To know what made him look like this.

But, before the feeling could grow, she stamped on it. She'd felt sympathy like this once too often, hadn't she? There was no way that she would ever become involved again. That was a path trodden only by fools.

Finally, he stopped staring at her and asked, 'What

are you doing here?' His voice was low. Husky, in a way that suddenly sent her pulses racing.

Trefor Dillon moved towards her, glancing through the open window. 'So!' he said. 'I take it you two have already met.'

'Yes.' Her voice was scarcely audible. 'Earlier this afternoon. On the mountain.'

CHAPTER TWO

SHOWERED and feeling ready to deal with anything or anyone—including the disturbing Dr Caswell—Eryl fished out the least crumpled of the summer dresses she had put into a weekend case with her night things. The rest of her luggage, still in the car now parked in the courtyard, could wait until later, she decided.

Trefor Dillon had told her to skip the emergency surgery tomorrow and ease herself into work on Monday. 'Spend Saturday looking around the area,' he'd said. 'Get the feel of the place. Some of it will seem very new to you.'

Now, slipping her feet into comfortable sandals and pulling on a flame-coloured dress she had picked up on impulse from a Birmingham market, she studied herself in a long mirror in the bathroom and wondered why on earth she had bought the thing in the first place.

In the Midlands it had seemed perfect. A bright spot against a perpetually grey background, it had given her a warm, cheerful feeling. But here it suddenly seemed too garish. Even though its tones didn't exactly scream against her russet hair, would it be suitable for supper with her new colleagues?

Unable to decide, she eventually told herself to stop dithering and kept it on. Then she began to brush hair that was still damp from the shower, pushing and pulling her natural curls into some sort of order. After outlining her mouth with pale lipstick, she applied a touch of grey eyeshadow and darkened her long lashes with mascara.

'You'll do!' she said to her reflection. Then, glancing at her watch and seeing that it was almost eight, she pulled a face and added, 'You'll just have to do. Come on! Get a move on, will you?'

As she dropped the key of the flat into her shoulder-bag she heard her front doorbell ring. Although it was not yet dark she touched a switch controlling the outside light, ready for when she returned, then fled down the stairs.

Expecting to see Trefor Dillon, Eryl smiled as she opened the door. 'How kind of you to. . .' she began. Then her smile faded abruptly.

It was Lewis Caswell who stood there. His dark hair, swept back from a high forehead, rested neatly against the collar of an immaculate grey suit. A deep blue shirt contrasted pleasingly with the pale grey of his silk tie.

Evening sunlight skimmed his face, accentuating the fine outline of high cheek-bones beneath tanned skin. A handsome face, she thought. Perhaps a little too handsome, with a mobile mouth just hovering on the edge of a smile. And those dark brown eyes, that this afternoon had been filled with fury, were now twinkling at her with something that looked very like amusement.

'Oh, it's you!' she said.

His smile grew. 'Yes, it's me. Not exactly bearing a bouquet of carefully selected flowers because there wasn't time. But at least offering an apology for my quick temper this afternoon.'

What game was he playing? He didn't seem the sort to say sorry for anything he'd done so she decided he was trying to flirt with her. But, just as she was about to say something sharp, she realised that he was quite

serious. Then she saw that strange loneliness come into
his eyes again and felt her heart softening so she smiled
back at him.

'Apology accepted,' she said quietly. 'I was as much
to blame.'

As he went on looking at her in silence she became
aware of a subtle magnetism in him. There was a broad-
ness of spirit there, too. A generosity that was pleasing.
But dangerous, she thought. It was this kind of magic
that had tripped her before and she knew she would
have to avoid it. Never again did she want to fall under
this sort of spell.

'I was rushing to an urgent case this afternoon,' he
said. 'But, even so, that doesn't excuse rudeness, does
it?' After looking at her thoughtfully for a moment
longer, he smiled again and asked, 'Will you allow me
to take you to supper?'

The invitation was as old-fashioned as Trefor
Dillon's had been and when he slipped a hand beneath
her elbow to guide her across the courtyard she felt as
if she had entered another world, where manners were
courteous and life gentle.

But she found his touch electric. Too tempting for
comfort, so she moved away. 'I can see where I'm
going perfectly well, thank you,' she said.

After that they walked to the house in silence and,
as she saw him frown, she silently cursed herself for
being churlish.

The food was simple. The kind of country fare she had
forgotten while she was in England but remembered
now with the same pleasure she had felt when Aunt
Maud had served up such meals years ago. In this very
dining-room, too.

There were cold pigs' trotters, slices of home-cured ham and Welsh lamb, accompanied by an enormous salad. Trefor told everyone with pride that he, himself, had grown the tomatoes, radishes and spring onions.

'To say nothing of these,' Mrs Reynolds said, placing a large dish of new potatoes on the table.

'They look delicious,' Eryl said. 'I love them tossed in melted butter and sprinkled with parsley like that.'

Mrs Reynolds sat at the table with them, serving the meat and looking at Eryl anxiously as if she feared criticism of her homely food.

'For goodness' sake, Martha!' Trefor Dillon exclaimed, sounding quite jovial despite his obvious irritation. 'Don't look so scared. Dr Thomas isn't going to eat you, along with your cooking.'

The woman pressed her lips together, staying silent as she handed the salad bowl to Eryl. Then, with a touch of humour, she said, 'I don't really think she would dare.'

Lewis Caswell laughed. 'So you've been giving her the treatment, have you? Well, let me warn you. Dr Thomas has a will of her own and quite a lively tongue.'

'I already know that. But I don't mind because she's Welsh. And lucky enough to have what we call *Hwyl*— the sort of inspiration others lack.' Now she turned to Eryl with the sweetest of smiles and said, 'I think we're going to get on fine together, Doctor. You must forgive me the little spat we had earlier on.'

So! The scene was now set for harmony, Eryl thought and glanced at Lewis, wondering how well she would get on with him. He was eyeing her with a look of amusement. Yet there was also a kind of calculation in his dark eyes, as if he was finding it difficult to weigh her up.

Good, she thought. Keep him guessing. The last thing she wanted was to get personally close to this man. There was no way that she would ever be more than professional with him.

When Mrs Reynolds left with their empty plates to fetch the next course from the kitchen, Trefor Dillon said to Eryl, 'It probably seems strange to you, having my housekeeper sitting at table with us.'

'Not at all. Why should it?'

He shrugged. 'Some people in this village would object if they'd been invited here.'

Eryl was amazed. 'What sort of people, for heaven's sake? Surely nobody's that snobbish!'

'You'd be surprised. The folk in Powys Manor, for instance.'

'You mean the Wynford-Wynnes? I find that hard to believe.'

The Wynne family had prided themselves on their descent from some ancient Welsh princeling, she remembered. They owned acres of land around here. To say nothing of the mountainside, which they'd leased to sheep farmers for generations. But, despite their wealth, they had never been standoffish.

'Oh, they've been long gone, I'm afraid.' The old doctor sighed. 'Sad, because they were splendid landlords. Real gentry. When the head of the family died the sons had to sell up to settle heavy death duties. Now a Yorkshireman, recently knighted for his contribution to industry, owns the lot and things are very different. There's no longer any sense of—togetherness, like there used to be. Sir George Wilson has no real feeling for the land, either. To him I'm afraid it's just a business.'

'He's a strange man,' Lewis said. 'Very antagonistic.

So just take care if you happen to cross his path.'

'That's hardly likely,' Trefor said. 'Although he's registered with us he never comes here. Pays a fortune for private medicine, I believe. Even has his own plane to take him to London.'

'Oh, well, each to his own taste,' Lewis said with a sigh. Then a dark frown creased his forehead. 'I can't say I approve. But at least his taxes are contributing to our National Health patients. And that means more care for them. Especially for the most needy people in our valley.'

Eryl looked at him with renewed interest. There seemed to be so many surprises in this man. First, the strange loneliness she had detected and now a very real sense of caring. At this moment her image of a playboy disappeared and she began to feel easier with him.

Mrs Reynolds returned with a tray loaded with plates and fruity Welshcakes, plus the most succulent trifle Eryl thought she had ever seen.

'This is a conspiracy to make us all fat,' she said, smiling at the housekeeper and now feeling more at home with her.

'A good thing, too!' Trefor exclaimed. 'You're as lean as a whippet, my girl. So just let Martha Reynolds feed you up a bit.'

When the meal was finished and they had lingered over coffee in the sitting-room, Eryl found that she could hardly keep her eyes open.

'Thank you for a wonderful supper,' she said. 'But I hope you'll forgive me if I leave now. It's been a long day.'

Lewis stood up. 'I'll walk you across,' he said.

'Thank you, but there's really no need. I've left the outside light on.'

But Trefor said, 'You will please allow Lewis to take you back. And, as I'm the boss around here, you'd better do as you're told!' His sharp words were tempered with that charming smile and Eryl found it impossible to object.

'Of course! Just as you say!' she said, teasing him gently.

'I'm quite serious,' he said. 'I know everything seems peaceful in this place but things are very different from when you used to live here. You really can't be too careful at night.'

She found this difficult to swallow but didn't attempt to argue with this wonderful old man.

As she went towards the courtyard with Lewis Caswell, she again avoided contact with him when he offered to take her arm. And long before they reached her front door she had delved into her bag for her key. After fitting it quickly into the lock and pushing the door open, she turned to thank him.

But the words didn't reach her lips. As the light shone on them both she found him staring at her with a puzzled frown. And his dark eyes seemed to be filled with unspoken questions.

'Yes?' she asked. 'What is it?'

He went on looking at her in silence for a while. But at last he sighed softly and said, 'It's nothing. Nothing at all. You—remind me a little of someone I once knew, that's all.'

Suddenly filled with embarrassment, she gave a breathless laugh. Trying to lighten the atmosphere, she said, 'Do I have such an ordinary face, then?'

'Oh, no. Not at all. It's a very beautiful face.'

She looked at him with suspicion, but he wasn't flirting with her. Nor was he flattering her. Rather, he seemed to be in a kind of dream. Remembering something out of his past, perhaps. Something that obviously gave him pain, by the stark look in his eyes.

She stayed quite still. Mesmerised. After a while he leant towards her and touched her cheek with a soft finger, drawing it down towards her chin and staring at her as if he couldn't believe she was real.

She desperately wanted to break away from his touch but she was afraid to move. Reluctant to disturb the thoughts going on behind those eyes in case—in some way she couldn't begin to understand—she brought him further pain.

At last his hand dropped to his side and he said, 'Goodnight!' and turned abruptly away from her, walking swiftly towards his car.

She went into the hall, half closed the door and stood peering through the narrow opening. Not until she saw him drive out of the courtyard and heard him turn into the road did she close the door, lock it and latch it with a chain. Then, walking slowly upstairs to the landing, she switched off the outside light.

What a strange mixture of a man he was, she thought. Angry at times. Blunt to the point of rudeness. Harsh one moment and caring the next. And deep inside there was a kind of wound. A sorrow that she had glimpsed but could not fathom. A sadness that could not be easily healed.

She snapped on her sitting-room light impatiently. You're a fool, she told herself. A stupid, over-sensitive fool. Concerning yourself with things that have nothing whatever to do with you. Looking beneath the surface of a man who is little more than a stranger to you. And

seeing pain there when most probably it just
doesn't exist.

After a restless night Eryl woke to birdsong and lay
listening to it with pleasure. Then last night's conversation over supper came back to her and again she was
appalled by the changes that had overtaken Dynas. Not
only was it exploding with caravans and ugly little
bungalows but the very core of it was in danger of
being shattered, and all because of death duties. With
the Wynford-Wynnes no longer owning the land, she
saw the community floundering, its heart destroyed by
a man of industry who didn't really care for his tenants.

As she began to wash and dress, this time in serviceable jeans and a summer top, she saw another picture
that disturbed her—of a doctor she did not want to
tangle with yet whose hidden depths intrigued her
despite herself.

Trying to stamp on these thoughts, she wandered
into the kitchen and found that some kind soul had
supplied a freshly baked loaf and a tin of ground coffee.
There was butter in the fridge and a jar of marmalade
in a cupboard over the worktops, but little else.

Deciding to spend some of her free Saturday shopping for food, she made coffee in a percolator, slipped
a slice of bread into a toaster and then spread it with
Welsh butter, refusing to spoil the wonderful taste with
marmalade. When she had eaten she left the wash-
ing-up in the sink and, picking up her shoulder-bag,
went into the courtyard where a large and elderly
Morris she didn't recognise was parked near her
own car.

Near some bushes by the front door was a grey cat
with long hair and orange eyes. It was staring at her as

if it was challenging her right to be there, Eryl thought.
She stooped down, holding out a friendly hand to the
animal, pleased when it came towards her. After rub-
bing its face against her fingers it gave a pitiful miaow.
And then, as if by magic, it was joined by four kittens,
all with different coloured coats.

'So, you're female, are you? And I suppose these
are your children,' Eryl said, not feeling at all foolish
talking like this to an animal.

The cat stared at her for a moment as if trying to
puzzle out what Eryl meant. 'So, you don't understand
English, is that it?' she asked. Stroking the soft fur, she
repeated what she had said in Welsh.

The cat immediately butted her hand and gave
another, louder miaow. Afterwards it lay on the ground,
begging to be stroked.

Eryl was still cooing softly and running her hands
through the cat's fur when she heard footsteps. Looking
up, she saw a young woman in nurse's uniform walking
towards her. Now feeling absolutely ridiculous, she
stood up and smiled, hoping that the nurse hadn't heard
her uttering such sentimental nonsense.

'Hi, there! I'm Nerys Powell, one of the nurses
attached to the surgery,' the girl said. 'And, no, don't
tell me! You can only be our new doctor.'

'Yes, that's right. I'm Eryl Thomas.'

'Do you make a habit of talking to animals?' the
young woman asked, her hazel eyes filling with amusement as she looked from Eryl to the cat.

'Quite often.' Eryl smiled back at her, liking her
immediately.

She was tall and slender, with tendrils of dark curly
hair escaping from her navy-blue uniform cap. Nerys
thrust out a hand, clasping Eryl's in a warm and friendly

grip. 'Welcome to the firm! It'll be good to have another female about the place,' she said. 'So, what do you think of our mystery cat?'

'She's very beautiful. But why do you call her a mystery?'

'Because that's just what she is. Nobody knows where she came from. She just turned up one day, bulging with unborn kittens, and dear old Dr Dillon couldn't bear to turn her away. Or have her put down, as someone suggested.'

'Oh, no! Who'd want to do a thing like that?'

'The housekeeper, would you believe! Can't stand furry creatures, she says.'

'So, where does the animal live?' Eryl asked.

'Oh, anywhere that's comfortable. But certainly not in the main house.'

'Has she got a name?'

'Yes, several. Ranging from "that dratted thing" to "hey you there"! On the quiet I've dubbed her Ladykins because she's so proud of her family and walks with a kind of royal dignity.'

'Then Ladykins it shall be. And from now on I'll take charge of her. She's welcome in my house. At least until her rightful owner claims her.'

'And that's not likely to happen. She's been here for weeks now. Even though we've advertised in shops. The local paper, too.'

'But she's a pedigree animal, isn't she?'

'Maybe. But even aristocrats can stray. As you must have noticed the moment you clapped eyes on her motley crew of kittens!' Nerys Powell laughed, walking towards the car Eryl had noticed earlier, then turned back to ask, 'D'you want a lift somewhere?'

'No, thanks. That's my car there, near yours. Dr

Dillon told me to look around Dynas before I start work on Monday so I thought I'd pop into the village. Do some shopping while I'm there.'

'I'm going that way so why not come with me? Anything to save petrol, I say.'

'You're sure? But what about getting back?'

'No problem. I've got to call here again, anyway. Promised to get Dr Dillon a magazine he wants.'

With that settled, the two of them set off together in Nerys's ancient car, which seemed to be crammed with everything but the kitchen sink.

'Sorry about all this,' Nerys said. 'I'm usually much smarter when I come to the surgery. I drive a neat little Fiat but it's being serviced at the moment. This is Doug's old crate.'

'Doug?'

'My husband, of all of six months!' Nerys gave a delightful laugh. Filled with sunshine, Eryl thought. Just like the girl herself. 'He's a farmer, hence all the junk in the back.'

'Mountain sheep?' Eryl enquired.

'No. Arable. With a few cows. On the other side of the valley. When we get to the car park near the old church I'll show you.'

They wound their way through streets crowded with Saturday shoppers, then turned into a square laid out with parking spaces and a slot machine for payment. As Nerys sprinted towards it as if she hadn't a moment to spare, Eryl looked about her, seeking landmarks that she might recognise. There were none and when Nerys returned, waving a ticket and saying that they would be safe for two hours, she found that she couldn't smile.

'What's wrong?' Nerys asked. 'You look as if you'd lost a fortune.'

'I—I think maybe I have.' Eryl tried to make a joke of it but the dull ache inside just wouldn't go away. 'I used to live here, you see. Long ago. But now—well, it's so changed. I feel as though I no longer belong.'

She didn't know why she was talking so frankly to this girl whom she'd only just met. Maybe it was because she was a stranger, she thought, and speaking to people you didn't really know was easier. A moment later she realised that it was because Nerys was showing all the signs of a good listener and was sympathetic without being maudlin.

'I see,' the nurse said quietly. 'I suppose, in a way, it must be like a bereavement.'

Perceptive. Friendly without being pushy. Perhaps even discreet enough to share confidences with? Eryl smiled, keeping these thoughts to herself. For now it was enough to have found a pleasant companion to go shopping with.

'Look!' Nerys said, pointing to some fields on the other side of the valley, back towards the surgery. 'See that rambling old farmhouse just beneath the hill? That's where Doug and I live. You must come and meet him some time.' She then gave Eryl a penetrating look and said, 'Now, I think Pam's Café is the order of the day. There's nothing like strong coffee to cheer you up.'

CHAPTER THREE

AFTER coffee, where Nerys relayed most of the local gossip which was amusing without being unkind, the two girls went shopping together. The first thing Eryl bought was a huge open-topped bag displayed in the window of Lloyd's, the general store she remembered from her early days. Woven from local rushes and lined with bright red material, it was ungainly but just what she needed, she decided.

She found the old shop reassuring for, apart from a lick of white paint here and there, it was the same as it had always been—even to the old-fashioned bell on a spring, which clanged loudly as the door opened. Certain that old Mr Lloyd would be long gone, she stared in disbelief when she saw him sitting behind the counter.

He looked up, a puzzled frown creasing his forehead. Then he said slowly, 'Don't I know you, *merchi bach*?'

Eryl smiled. It was a long time since she had been called 'little girl' in Welsh, which was used as a term of endearment.

'Eryl Thomas,' she said, holding out her hand to him. 'Your new doctor.'

Taking her hand, he shook his head in wonder and said, 'Well, well!' This was followed by a stream of local Welsh dialect.

Fishing deep into her early memories, Eryl found that she could reply quite easily in the same tongue. She talked with him for a while before leaving with

32

the new shopping bag, followed by Nerys who was now filled with admiration.

'How come you speak not just ordinary Welsh but the same language as the locals?' she asked.

Eryl smiled. 'It's easy. After all, my family lived in this valley for generations.'

'You'll probably find that an advantage in your work,' Nerys said, with just the faintest hint of envy. 'Me, I've had to try hard for recognition in this place. But I think I can now say they've begun to accept me. Specially since I married one of their own precious sons!'

They had come to a modern-looking mini-market and, as they went in, Eryl wondered if being born here really was an advantage. She wasn't certain. It could work the other way round, couldn't it? She was sure that there would be times when she wished to remain anonymous. When she didn't want people from her past to remember too much about her. Things that could still hurt.

As she pushed a trolley through the aisles, filling it with food to stock her fridge and cupboards and tins of cat food for Ladykins—while Nerys picked up the magazine for Trefor—she asked if Lewis Caswell had found it difficult to fit in here.

'At first he did,' Nerys said. 'In fact, at one point he nearly left. But that was when he'd just started. People found him standoffish and thought he was trying to be superior.'

'He's different now, I take it.'

Nerys grinned at her. 'Sometimes. But he's still got much to learn. Though, mind you, I think shyness has a lot to do with it.'

'He seems to have his fair share of anger too,' Eryl

said. 'Almost as if life has let him down in some way.'

Nerys shrugged. 'Yes, he can be moody. But I don't really know why. He's such a loner, you see. Draws back the moment anyone gets too near. Especially women. Maybe he once had a disastrous love affair.'

The young nurse smiled as if she didn't really believe this and Eryl began to worry about their lack of discretion. The first day, she thought, and here she was gossiping like an old crone. 'Perhaps we should forget this conversation,' she suggested as they walked to the check-out, 'before we get accused of being unprofessional.'

Nerys grinned wickedly. 'It's Saturday,' she declared. 'The time when you can let your tongue run away with you.'

'But even so. . .'

As Eryl opened her purse to pay, Nerys said, 'You mustn't worry, love. I'm usually as silent as the grave when it comes to my colleagues. And my patients, of course. That goes without saying.'

Eryl looked at the girl's open smile and decided that she liked her even more than she had at first. 'Good,' she said. 'The same goes for me.'

They returned to the car park, carrying the heavy bag between them. 'You've bought enough to last a month,' Nerys said as they dumped it on the ground. 'What a good job you came with me. How else would you have carried all this?'

'It was brilliant using your car, too. I've just remembered I haven't finished unloading my luggage yet.'

It was when they were carrying the groceries to her flat that Eryl noticed Lewis Caswell's car parked in the courtyard. She was certain that it hadn't been there when she'd left.

Nerys caught her puzzled look and said, 'It's a mystery to me, too. When Dr Dillon and I covered emergencies this morning he told me Lewis had gone to Dolgelly on some private business or other.' They dropped the bag by Eryl's flat and Nerys said, 'I think I'll just pop into the surgery and find out what's going on.'

After unlocking the door of her flat and pushing the bag inside, Eryl followed her, only to see Lewis coming across the courtyard, his stethoscope slung around his neck and a frown darkening his face.

'Thank God you're here!' he said, taking her arm and hurrying her towards the surgery block.

'Why? What's happened?'

'It's Trefor. He's collapsed.'

Nerys went in with them and they found the old doctor lying on a couch in his own surgery, with Mrs Reynolds hovering over him. His face was pale and he looked weak. But, in spite of this, he kept trying to sit up, with the housekeeper pushing him back again and telling him in Welsh that it was time he did as he was told for a change.

'Mrs Reynolds! I asked you to sit with him, not manhandle him like this!' Lewis's voice was sharp but failed to hide an underlying anxiety. 'You can go now that Dr Thomas is here. And, while you're about it, perhaps you would be good enough to open the gates to the surgery block.'

As Mrs Reynolds scuttled out he turned to Eryl, explaining that he'd rung for an ambulance and had been about to open the gates himself when he'd seen her.

'What happened?' Nerys asked. 'He was OK when I did surgery with him earlier. If I'd seen any signs of this I'd have done something about it at once.'

'Of course you would. I know that.' Lewis smiled, reassuring her. 'He'd asked me to call into the house on my way back from Dolgelly to discuss something. He wasn't there so I came to the surgery on the off chance. At first he seemed OK until he suddenly felt weak.'

'And I'm all right now,' Trefor said, trying to sit up, only to sink back again.

'Of course you are,' Lewis said, surprising Eryl with the gentle compassion that she heard in his voice. 'We just want to make sure, that's all. So we're sending you to the cottage hospital in Pandy. Just for a checkup.'

Trefor groaned. 'I hate all hospitals! Especially that one! So just be warned, will you? I'll refuse to stay!'

Nerys smiled at him. 'That's the spirit, Doctor! You give them what for! But please remember they'll only be trying to help.'

'Huh! With a starvation diet, no doubt!' The old man's voice trailed away and he shut his eyes, suddenly too weary to go on with any more invective.

Eryl moved away, saying quietly to Lewis, 'Is it his heart?'

'I thought so at first. But when I examined him I wasn't sure. I could see no obvious signs. No cyanosis, for instance. The only pallor was in the face. I couldn't detect anything going on inside, either.' He handed her his stethoscope. 'Listen to his chest yourself, will you? Tell me what you think.'

She did as he suggested, listening for the classic signs of heart failure, but could detect nothing. The pumping action of the ventricle sounded normal so she scanned his face, searching for traces of sweat that she might have missed. But she found none. Taking the instrument from her ears, she took Lewis aside and asked, 'Where was the initial pain?'

'That's what's so puzzling. He says there was none at all. Just a general sensation of weakness, making him unable to stand any longer.'

The sound of an ambulance arriving interrupted their quiet conversation. There was so much that she still wanted to ask. If this had ever happened to Dr Dillon before. What the man's general health had been like in the past. And perhaps, more importantly, what was the real reason for him giving up a sizeable portion of his work?

She also found herself inordinately curious about the discussion that Lewis had expected to have with Dr Dillon. Was it connected with his visit to Dolgelly? As two paramedics came in with a stretcher, she told herself that it had nothing to do with her. Private business, Nerys had said. So, what was she doing giving it even a second thought?

'Thanks for your help, Dr Thomas,' Lewis said, addressing her formally in front of the ambulance crew as they took the stretcher out. 'There's no need for you to do anything more. Nurse Powell and I will travel with him to the hospital.'

'Oh, but. . .'

'There's really no need for you to bother.'

'But I'd like to come,' she said, hoping that she sounded firm but not argumentative. 'It'll be a chance for me to see the hospital before I begin work.'

'It's a good idea, Dr Caswell,' Nerys offered. 'I really should get home. We're expecting visitors this afternoon.'

He shrugged. 'Just as you wish.'

Ten minutes later the ambulance was going over the last of the hills to Pandy and Eryl suddenly wished that she hadn't offered to come. The very sight of the place would bring back dark memories, she was sure. But when they were nearing the hospital that had not been there in her day she realised that this village had changed as much as Dynas. Even the surgery where Robert Davies had worked had altered out of all recognition.

For a moment she let her thoughts stray to the first and only man whom she had ever really loved. She remembered her naïvety of those days. Her simple trust that had made her believe Robert when he'd told her she was the only woman for him. And how she had seen a magic life opening up in front of her. She had been a medical student at Guy's then, working towards the extra qualification needed for general practice. She had been on holiday and visiting the surgery in Pandy because her father had told her to.

'It won't do you much good watching me in Dynas all the time,' he'd said. 'Spread your wings a bit. Try all the surgeries round here. I'll give you all the necessary introductions.'

After seeing several other places, she had finally attached herself to a three-man surgery in Pandy, finding Dr Robert Davies's guidance just what she'd needed. She'd thought she had also needed his love.

The ambulance turned into a yard and drew up in front of the hospital's main entrance and she was swept along with the crew. Lewis leant against the reception desk, talking earnestly to a young man she later learnt was Dr Smith, a registrar attached to the general hospital in Swanton, a small town near the coast.

'We're lucky to have found him,' Lewis said, after introducing her. 'He shares duties between this place and Swanton. Today it just happens to be Pandy's turn.'

They went into an examination room, where Trefor Dillon was put through preliminary tests before being attached to a heart monitor. After looking closely at the screen for a few moments even Eryl, as a non-specialist, could see that it told them precisely nothing, except that Trefor seemed to be in excellent health.

So she wasn't surprised when Dr Smith, leaving Trefor with a nurse in charge, took them both into another room and said, 'It's a puzzle, I must admit. Just as you first said.'

'What do you propose we should do?' Lewis asked.

'Leave him here for a while. I'd like to do further tests, if that's all right with you. I specialise in coronary medicine but I'd also like to bring in a colleague who's doing some research into early symptoms of diabetes.'

'I hadn't thought of that, I must admit,' Lewis said, looking annoyed with himself.

'I'm not surprised. He presents as a typical heart case but without the pain. So, what on earth is one to make of that?' The man then turned to Eryl and asked her what she thought.

She immediately remembered treating a woman in the Midlands who had collapsed in much the same way. When the patient was sent to the Queen Elizabeth Hospital in Birmingham, presumably with an early coronary, in the end it had turned out that she was suffering from sheer exhaustion.

Now timid of suggesting this, but nevertheless determined to speak, she said, 'It couldn't be simply that Dr Dillon has been overdoing things, could it? Perhaps sleeping badly because of overwork.'

Lewis gave her a puzzled look. 'That doesn't really seem likely. Unless you've noticed something I've missed. If so. . .'

'I've met this sort of thing before. In Birmingham. It sounds too simple to be true, I know. But. . .'

'Your colleague may have a point there, Dr Caswell,' the registrar said. 'Sometimes we doctors are too full of specialist explanations to see clearly. You may well be right, Dr Thomas. Tell me about the case you mentioned.'

Eryl explained about her patient and at last Lewis lost his puzzled look. He even said that he, too, remembered dealing with a similar case.

'Where?' Eryl asked.

'In Africa,' he said. Then, seeing her surprise, he added, 'I did a stint there with the World Health Organisation.'

She was silent, suddenly filled with an admiration that she hadn't expected to feel. She also registered the fact that the tan that she'd thought he had acquired on some exotic beach was probably left over from working beneath the fierce African sun. Quite suddenly she was ashamed of that thought and looked at him with new eyes.

He caught her gaze and smiled at her, as if he had read what was going on in her mind. And she saw a strange warmth in him and didn't know how to deal with it so she looked away. Yet she couldn't ignore a very real magnetism that seemed to be drawing her towards him in spite of herself.

At last, with Trefor settled into one of three single wards of which this cottage hospital was justifiably proud, Eryl and Lewis left together. Silently because there seemed to be nothing to say.

From time to time she caught him glancing at her as if he was trying to unravel her thoughts. And she was aware of a strange magnetic current between them, drawing her mind towards his. It was so strange, she thought. Just as if she was able to touch his spirit in some way and was even beginning to understand the enigma that seemed to be such a large part of him.

She gave a little involuntary shiver. She didn't want to acknowledge what was happening to her. Didn't want her life to become complicated like this. She told herself firmly that all she was experiencing was a kind of physical attraction. And she could definitely do without that. There was no way that she would ever make a fool of herself over a man who was little more than a stranger. Besides, she was pretty certain that he felt nothing for her. It was just his curiosity that made him look at her like this.

It was when they reached the street that they both realised that they had no transport because they had arrived in the ambulance.

'So, what do we do now?' Lewis asked, suddenly looking so tired that she wanted to reach out her hands to him. 'Find a taxi?'

'You mean they've at last got round to such things here?'

'I don't really know. I've never had to use one.'

'There's always a bus, I suppose. Though when I lived in the area I remember it took ages to find one.'

They began to walk along the pavement, searching for anything that looked remotely like a bus stop. Then suddenly Eryl was overcome by helpless laughter.

'What's so funny?' Lewis asked.

'We are. We must look like tourists, walking because

we enjoy it. When all the time I, for one, would rather
be taking it easy over a cup of tea.'

'Well, then, why don't we do just that? Come on!
There must be a café somewhere.'

Before she knew it Lewis had taken her arm and was
whisking her down a side street to a little shop with
bull's-eye windows.

'Here we are! Just what the doctor ordered,' he said
as he marched her in and sat her at a table for two
covered by a crisp gingham cloth. 'Tea or coffee?'

'Tea, please.'

'And cakes?'

'Lovely.' Eryl could imagine nothing better. Lunchtime had come and gone and she was starving.

The place was empty but a long curtain at the back
of the room twitched and an elderly waitress arrived.
She was dressed in native Welsh costume, presumably
for the benefit of tourists.

Eryl hadn't felt so carefree for ages. As she sat back
and relaxed, she smiled at Lewis. Perhaps working with
this man would be easier than she had first thought.
True, at times he seemed withdrawn but at others he
could be surprisingly pleasant. Like now, when he was
relaxed. He was leaning towards her and asking her
questions about her work in the Midlands, even touching on other subjects such as her interests outside
medicine. And all the time his expressive eyes were
looking straight into hers, concentrating on her, with
no hint of flirtation.

Oh, yes, he would be a good colleague. Someone
whose company she could enjoy without fear—if she
could ignore the growing attraction she felt.

It was when they had left the café and were walking
along the main road in search of a bus stop that a car

drew up alongside them. It was a Bentley, sleek and immaculate. And driving it was a smartly groomed woman with shining black hair, wearing a lightweight grey suit that positively shouted Dior.

She leaned through the open window, looking straight at Lewis as she said, 'Hi there! I think you forgot to take this when you left.' She handed him a book and a pair of deep blue eyes twinkled at him as her mouth stretched into a tantalising smile.

Eryl felt as if she had become invisible and that Lewis and this woman were the only people in the street. And, suddenly, that wonderful moment of comradeship vanished.

'Where were you going?' Lewis asked.

'To your cottage to return what you left behind.'

'Great!' he said. 'I'm without a car at the moment so could you possibly give us a lift?'

'Of course. Hop in.' Now she noticed Eryl for the first time, and said, 'Aren't you going to introduce your friend?'

'My colleague,' he corrected swiftly. 'Meet the new addition to our surgery, Dr Thomas.' He turned to Eryl and said, 'This is Jennifer Vaughan.'

The introductions complete, with Eryl none the wiser about this very beautiful woman who seemed to be as rich as Croesus, Jennifer Vaughan then drove over the hills to Dynas. Eryl sat in the back because Jennifer said that she wanted Lewis near her as they had some business to discuss.

What it was, and exactly who the woman was, Eryl didn't manage to find out because the two of them spoke too quietly for her to catch even a stray word. As if they wanted to be private, she thought. And she certainly didn't want to intrude.

When they reached a row of cottages Jennifer slowed down but Lewis asked her to go on to the surgery.

'Why not drop you here?' the woman asked, sounding distinctly put out.

'Because Dr Thomas lives in the stable flat there.'

'Tell you what! Why don't I deliver her there first, then take you to your cottage?'

'No need, Jennifer. My own car's parked outside the surgery.'

'Pity about that. I thought taking you home would give us a chance to talk further. Our earlier meeting was so rushed, wasn't it?'

Eryl glanced in the driving mirror as Jennifer drove on. That beautiful smile was back on the woman's face; those deep blue eyes were twinkling again. And there was a strange feeling of emptiness in Eryl's heart.

She suddenly recognised it as envy and hated herself for it. What was she doing, feeling like this? The woman might be perfection itself. Might even be in the middle of a torrid relationship with Lewis. Whatever. Neither of these two people meant anything to her. So why this stab of jealousy?

Jennifer drew up in front of the old house. As Eryl and Lewis got out of the car, the woman asked, 'Are you sure you wouldn't like me to follow you home? It's time you treated me to coffee instead of always drinking mine!'

Lewis stood on the pavement, looking at her for a moment, his face expressing nothing. Then he said, 'Some other time, perhaps. There's no real hurry to get this thing settled, is there?'

'No, I suppose not.'

As the woman waved and sped off, Eryl wondered what on earth they were talking about. Then she told herself that it had absolutely nothing to do with her.

She thanked Lewis for the tea and went towards her flat, not expecting him to come with her. But when she found him by her side she felt obliged to ask him in.

But he just smiled, saying, 'That's kind. But no, thanks. I'm rather busy at the moment.' Then, taking her key from her, he opened her front door to let her in.

The gesture of a true gentleman, she thought, and knew that it should have pleased her. But it didn't. Instead, it left her with an odd feeling of depression.

Now she was even more puzzled by this strange man. For as she watched him walk towards his car he seemed preoccupied. As if, since meeting Jennifer Vaughan, a great weight had shifted itself onto his shoulders.

CHAPTER FOUR

ON MONDAY morning Eryl found herself unusually nervous. With no Dr Dillon to guide her on her first day everything would be up to her. Fitting herself into an unknown routine, finding out where everything was kept and, above all, keeping her head when she came into contact with Lewis Caswell was daunting, to say the least. She also found herself giving far too much thought to the woman he had introduced as Jennifer Vaughan. Who was she? And why had she found it so necessary to talk to him in hushed tones? Was she a spectre from a past he would prefer to hide?

Suddenly annoyed with her thoughts, she tried to pull herself together. Whatever Dr Caswell did with his spare time was nothing to do with her. This sort of snooping was more suited to a gangling schoolchild than to a doctor with dreams of adding 'FRCP' to her name one day.

Picking up her medical bag from the hall table, she locked the door of a now tidy flat behind her. Then, conscious of looking her best in a light blue summer suit with a white short-sleeved blouse beneath the jacket, she walked into the courtyard.

Telling herself to hold onto her confidence, she remembered what her father had said to her when she and Robert had split up, and stood a little straighter.

'When you're down—maybe right at rock bottom— climb up again at once,' he'd said. 'That way you'll reach even higher peaks than before.'

And again, just before he'd died of a massive stroke, he'd told her that when she found herself alone, strength would come to her if she looked for it.

'You'll always find the courage to go on,' he'd said, his voice almost too weak to be heard. 'For that's the way of the Thomas family.'

And all this was spoken with such love, even though he must have been so sad for her. Not just because of Robert but also because of what she had done.

Now, holding her head high, she opened the door of the surgery block and walked past the waiting area where a number of patients were sitting reading magazines. They glanced at her curiously as she went on to Reception, where two women were already pulling patients' notes from a row of pigeon-holes.

One of them looked up when Eryl arrived, smiled and asked, 'Can I help you?'

'I hope so. I'm the new GP. Dr Dillon was going to introduce me today but. . .'

'Oh, yes, we heard. Terrible thing to happen so suddenly,' the woman said.

'How is he? Have you had any news?' the other woman asked.

At that moment Dr Caswell appeared from his own surgery. 'I've just phoned the hospital in Pandy,' he said. 'Staff Nurse tells me Dr Dillon's had a peaceful night. I plan to visit him later.' He gave Eryl a professional sort of smile and said, 'Now, let me introduce you to our two receptionists. Meet Glynis Jones and Betty Williams. They'll tell you all you need to know about arrangements and so on.' He then went back to his surgery and Eryl smiled hopefully at the two women behind the desk.

Glynis was the woman who'd already greeted her.

Middle-aged, large and cheerful with a kindly eye, she shook Eryl's hand warmly and said, 'That's right, Doctor. We're here to help all comers.'

Betty Williams was younger. Slim and wiry, with a serious expression that looked as if it could become off-putting, Eryl saw her being useful when dealing with difficult patients.

'These are your morning patients,' she said, handing Eryl a list of names. 'I'll bring their notes to your surgery when I've finished collecting them. The computer on your desk is quite simple to use and contains information on all patients registered here. If it's not the kind you've met before give me a buzz and I'll help you.'

Eryl thanked her and turned to move away.

Then Glynis Jones said, 'The coat! Don't forget that.' She dived beneath the desk and produced a new white jacket wrapped in Cellophane. Casting an eye over Eryl, she said, 'A good fit, I'd say.'

Eryl took it, looking at it doubtfully. 'In my last practice we wore our ordinary clothes,' she said.

Glynis smiled at her. 'That was there but this is here,' she said, looking wise, as if she was uttering a piece of philosophy by which all Welsh doctors were expected to live. Then she leant towards her—one woman confiding in another. 'It's Dr Dillon, see. He likes the old ways best, with women doctors what he calls "suitably dressed", bless him! So who are we to argue?'

At last, sitting on a swivel chair behind a large oak desk facing the door, Eryl switched on the computer which was similar to the one she'd worked with in the Midlands. It recorded patients' treatment and prescriptions, along with details of age and so on. After touching various keys on the board, she brought up names to match those on her list.

Glancing at her watch, she saw that she had ten minutes to go before surgery began and decided to move her desk so that she would have more contact with patients. After trying to lift one end of it without success, she went into Reception.

'Does anyone feel strong enough to shift some furniture?' she asked.

Glynis Jones gaped at her and said, 'What do you want to move? And why?'

'It's the desk. I feel—hemmed in.'

'But the other doctors always receive their patients like that. I should have thought. . .'

'Is something wrong?' Betty Williams glanced up from a sheaf of papers she was sorting and frowned.

What a wonderful way to begin the first day, Eryl thought, wanting to kick herself. Then Lewis Caswell came out of his surgery, asking what all the fuss was about.

Wishing that she could vanish like a character in a fairy story, Eryl forced herself to face him. 'It's quite simple, really. I just want someone to help me move that heavy desk in there. Is it too much to ask?'

'I was saying, Doctor. . .' Glynis began.

'It doesn't matter what you were saying, Mrs Jones. If Dr Thomas wants to rearrange her surgery she's perfectly at liberty to do so. And don't worry, I'll lend her a hand.'

Amazed by his generosity and pleased with his professional loyalty, Eryl followed Lewis as he strode towards her room.

'Tell me where you want the desk, will you?'

'Just set at an angle, I suppose. So that I don't feel

so separated from the patients. Or—how about moving it under the window, with me sitting in front of it?' She cocked her head on one side, narrowing her eyes to take in the whole scene. 'When the door opens I can always swivel round. And if that small wooden chair that's in front of the desk now is placed beside mine for the patient I'll have direct access.'

He frowned at her. 'Have you thought it through properly? Is it wise?'

She was puzzled. 'Wise? What d'you mean?'

He studied her for a moment, a serious expression darkening his face. 'Doctors sometimes need protection from patients is what I mean. Surely you know this from your last practice?'

She laughed. 'You make this place sound like Rampton or Broadmoor.'

'I'm not joking, Eryl,' he said. 'Working anywhere these days can be a risk. Trefor must have warned you, surely.'

'Only by saying that Dynas had changed and telling me to be careful the night we had supper with him. But I didn't take it seriously.'

He looked at her with a trace of irritation. 'Then you should, Doctor. Myself, I wouldn't dream of sitting in front of a piece of furniture that could offer even a small amount of protection.'

She didn't believe she was hearing this. 'Have you ever been attacked?' she asked.

'No, thank God! But there's been some trouble in Pandy. Drug thefts and so on. If I were you I'd keep the desk where it is so that at least you can guard the drugs cupboard behind you.'

This seemed to make sense at last so she gave in, deciding not to move the desk for the moment. 'But if

I find it too awkward I may change my mind,' she said.

'Of course. The choice is yours. But just take care, that's all. And if you do find you're in trouble for heaven's sake remember to use that alarm button at the end of the desk.' A slow smile spread over his face and, before going out, he said, 'We don't want to lose our new partner, you know.'

They were heart-warming words, spoken with sincerity but, nevertheless, a typical remark made by one professional to another. As she watched him turn towards the door she wished that she had heard something else in his voice. A warmth because he, himself, wanted her to be here. Then she told herself not to be so foolish. What did it matter how he felt about her? She was here to do a job. To work with him, not to examine every nuance in his voice.

The moment he left Betty Williams came in, placing a pile of envelope folders containing patient notes on the desk. 'I've arranged them in order of appointment. The first one at the top,' she said. Then she glanced meaningfully at the desk. 'I see it's still where it was. Couldn't Dr Caswell lift it, after all?'

'Oh yes, of course he could. But he persuaded me not to move it.'

The woman's eyebrows lifted as a smile flitted across her face. 'That figures!' she said. 'Our dear Lewis usually gets his own way.'

Eryl detected amusement at Lewis's expense and as a colleague—and a very new one at that—her loyalty was quick to show itself. 'He was quite right,' she said.

'So you agreed without making a fuss?'

Eryl looked curiously at her. She had thought the woman's sharpness might be useful when it came to dealing with difficult patients but she didn't like the way it seemed to be directed against Lewis. 'There was nothing to make a fuss about,' she said. 'So will you be good enough to send in my first patient, please?'

She should probably not have spoken so severely to the receptionist on her first day here but she just didn't care. However prickly Lewis Caswell might be, at least he deserved professional loyalty.

The first patient to enter was Mrs West, a woman going through a difficult menopause and who was waiting for hormone replacement therapy. According to her notes she was eager to begin the programme but had delayed because her husband didn't trust what he called 'these newfangled treatments'.

'Would you like me to talk to him?' Eryl suggested.

'Well—perhaps,' the woman said, glancing nervously at the door.

'Is he waiting for you in Reception?' Eryl asked, thinking that she would invite him in to discuss any problem now.

'Oh, no! I came alone. Quite alone.'

Her voice shook and Eryl wondered if the man himself was causing her to look so scared then decided that a meeting with the husband would be a good move. Not only could she persuade him that this was by far the best treatment for his wife but she could also look for deeper reasons for the fear that she saw in her. In her past experience with women who had looked like this she had sometimes uncovered a whole history of ill-treatment.

'I would really like to meet him,' Eryl said gently.

'If—if you think that's best. Then, yes, I'll try to persuade him.'

That wasn't good enough so Eryl spoke more firmly. 'I would want to see you both together. May I suggest you book an appointment for the two of you on your way out? For about a week from now. But you must make sure he attends.'

'Of course, Doctor. I will. And thank you.'

Now that the decision had been taken out of her hands the woman looked relieved. As she left Eryl noticed with satisfaction that her walk was already more sprightly.

After entering notes into the computer, quickly duplicating them on the envelope files for back-up, Eryl called in the second patient of the day. This was young Charlie Daniels, a schoolboy of thirteen with a perpetually runny nose, who seemed to spend most of his term-time at home. He came in reluctantly with his mother, who drew up a second chair and sat close to him as if she feared that he might bolt.

Eryl examined his throat and ears, pulled down one lower eyelid to check the colour at the base of the eye and decided that he wasn't any more anaemic than any other teenager going through a period of rapid growth. Then she listened to his chest. Finding nothing dramatic there, she wondered if the cause of his excessive catarrh might be psychological.

'I don't know what to do with him, Doctor,' his mother said when Eryl straightened up, hanging her stethoscope around her neck. 'These head colds always seem to come out of the blue, so to speak.'

'At any particular time of year, would you say?'

'No, any time. That's what's so funny. I got really worried the other day, though. There was a TV programme about a child with the same symptoms as our Charlie. At first the doctors couldn't find a thing wrong with him. Yet there this kid was, snuffling just the same

as my lad. In the end they put it down to some rare
allergy.'

'Well, we could arrange tests for Charlie if you like.'

Mrs Daniels stared at Eryl for a moment. Then, leaning towards her, she said in a low voice, 'I had my own
ideas about that boy on TV.'

'Oh, yes? And what were they?'

Mrs Daniels began to look frightened and lowered
her voice even more as she said, 'Drugs, Doctor. D'you
think it could be that with my Charlie?'

In spite of the whispering Charlie overheard and
protested loudly with a stream of not very polite Welsh.
Eryl frowned, waiting for him to calm down.

When he subsided, giving her a sulky look, she asked
quietly, 'Have you ever sniffed glue, Charlie? Or swal-
lowed anything you don't want your mother to know
about? You'd better tell me the truth. Because if I
think you're lying I can easily give you some tests and
find out.'

He stared back at her defiantly. 'I never done any-
thin' like that, see! Preacher says it's bad. So I
wouldn't.'

Surprised, Eryl said, 'You go to church, then?'

'Chapel. Belong to the youth club an' all.'

'Oh, yes, he's a good boy is our Charlie,' Mrs
Daniels said. 'But, then, you never know these days,
do you?' She paused, looking thoughtfully at the wall
opposite, and then came out with, 'The funny thing is he
gets worse when there's a special project on at school.
D'you think that might have something to do with it?'

So, her guess may have been right, Eryl thought,
remembering all the other little wretches in the
Midlands who played hookey when they found the
work too hard. After a while they would present a

whole variety of very real symptoms that disguised the root cause.

'It's possible,' she said. 'Have you spoken to his teacher about him? Asked how he's getting on? If there's a subject he finds specially difficult?'

The woman hadn't been near the school so Eryl did her best to persuade her to visit Charlie's teacher as soon as possible. Then she recommended a course of vitamins to build up the boy's general health.

'I'm afraid I can't prescribe them,' she said. 'But you can buy them over the counter at any chemist. If he's no better when he's finished the tablets make another appointment to see me and, if I think it necessary, we'll arrange a session with an ear, nose and throat specialist.'

'Probe every cause you can think of,' her professor of medicine had said when she was training. Words that she thought she would remember until the end of her days.

And so the morning went on with a wide spectrum of patients to be seen but not so many in one session as there had been in the Midlands. When the last patient left Eryl leaned back in her chair and stretched, feeling contented.

Yes, this had been a wise move, she decided. Now, instead of having to act like a factory hand she could be a real doctor, with time to devote to patients who were people instead of being mere commodities.

At lunchtime she took off her white coat, hanging it on the back of the door, ready to slip across to her flat. Because it was her first day she had no visits this afternoon so she decided to relax in the peace of her new home. As she was passing Reception she caught sight of Nerys Powell and invited her to share a snack with her.

'Sorry, no can do,' the girl said, then introduced another woman in nurse's uniform. 'Meet Liz Brown. We share the work here, besides taking turns with district visiting. We also run various clinics in the treatment room.'

Eryl approved of Liz Brown, just as she had Nerys Powell, and silently congratulated Trefor on his choice of staff. Liz was a complete contrast to Nerys. Plump, with mouse-coloured, fly-away hair and a round face that dimpled when she smiled, her brown eyes shone with amusement as if the world she lived in was full of laughter.

'Hi! Glad to meet you,' she said warmly. 'Sorry, can't stop now but I'll catch up with you later. Injections to sort out before the hordes arrive.'

With that, she whisked away and Eryl laughed. 'Is she always in such a hurry?'

'Tell me about it!' Nerys said. 'By the way, how did you get on at the hospital on Saturday? Any news of the patient?'

'Dr Caswell says he's comfortable. But that could mean anything, couldn't it?'

Then Lewis himself was there, coming from his surgery on silent feet and startling her as he said, 'Why don't you see for yourself? This afternoon. I've got just one visit to do and then I'm off to Pandy. Why don't you come with me?'

However much she was looking forward to a peaceful afternoon, Eryl felt that she couldn't refuse. In the short time that she had been there she had grown genuinely fond of the old man and really wanted to visit him.

'Thanks,' she said, handing her patient envelopes to

Betty Williams. Taking her medical bag with her as they both walked out of the building, she asked, 'But what about lunch first? Would you like to share a snack with me?'

'Great! But not in your flat. In my cottage, if you don't mind. I've got some smoked salmon in the fridge that's much too good to waste.' As she hesitated he said, 'Oh, come on, Doctor! Even though I think it's time we got to know each other better I don't have any plans to molest you!'

She laughed. 'Your car or mine?'

'That, if I may say so, sounds highly suggestive.'

He grinned at her and she suddenly felt light-hearted, preferring his humour to the over-cautious attitude of this morning when he was refusing to move her desk.

In the courtyard she caught sight of Ladykins coming towards her, greeting her with a little chirrup as her kittens followed. She said, 'Will you wait while I dump my medical bag and feed my cat?'

'*Your* cat? I thought she was a stray.'

'She was. But no longer. I've adopted her. And her four kittens, I'll have you know.'

He gave her a helpless look, then burst out laughing. 'As if you hadn't enough to do round here already. By the way, I hear your morning patients liked you. Glynis told me.'

Smiling, Eryl unlocked the door to let in her new family of five cats. 'Just give me time to open a tin, will you?'

'Why don't you bring the food down here? You don't really have time to wait for the whole of that zoo to eat. And you don't want to shut them in, do you?'

'Right. Won't be long.' Putting her medical case on the hall table but keeping her bag still slung over her shoulder she hurried upstairs. After ladling cat meat into a bowl and pouring milk into a saucer, she took them to the courtyard.

Lewis was squatting on the ground, stroking Ladykins and talking quietly to the kittens. Eryl stayed quite still, watching him and trying to slot yet another side of a complicated character into the man who seemed to have so many facets.

When she at last set the dishes down and shut her door Lewis stood up, laughing as he said, 'I'm glad I never became a vet. At least people can tell you what they feel when they're ill.'

'Not always,' she said.

'You ought to have a cat flap,' Lewis remarked, as they went to his car and he opened the passenger door for her. 'We'll suggest it to Trefor, if you like. Ask his permission to mistreat his door.' He slid in beside her and started the engine. 'If he agrees you can get Gareth Pugh's son, Gwillim, to fix it for you. That's the family I plan to visit before I give you lunch. They're sheep farmers.'

'I think I know them,' Eryl said as he drove to the main road. 'At least, I used to visit a Pugh family with my father when I was a small child. It was a special treat, going with him on his rounds. Especially there, right to the top of the mountains. I used to think we were driving to heaven! Later we became close friends with the family.'

'Sounds like the same people. Elderly parents, Mair and Gareth. Three grown-up children still at home. Gwillim, who's the youngest, Ellen and Llew. The parents never left the area, except to go to hospital when Gareth was gored by a bull. Before my time here, of course.'

'I remember that accident! So these really must be the people I knew.' Eryl sat quietly, thinking back to those distant days with an ache of nostalgia. 'They've been here as long as time itself.'

They were driving up a rutted path towards a white-washed farmhouse when Lewis said, 'You being here with me could make things much easier. If you could talk to them, I mean. They'll probably accept you because you were born here. So far I've met nothing but resistance from the old man.'

'What's wrong with him?'

'An enlarged prostate. He really ought to see a specialist but I just can't persuade him.'

'What treatment are you giving him?'

'Oh, the usual anti-inflammatory drugs, which I suspect he's lax about taking.'

'Have you tried talking to his wife? Or the rest of the family? I should have thought Ellen and her brothers would be receptive.'

'But they're so damned uncommunicative.'

'I expect that's because they don't often speak English.'

'Really? In this day and age?'

'Oh, yes. This used to be called the forgotten valley. When they were children all school lessons were in Welsh, with English as a foreign language they could learn if they wanted. But they never used it at home.'

'You amaze me!'

Eryl smiled, then went on to tell him everything she could remember of the family. 'Ellen, who's quite a bit older than me, was once married, you know. Even moved out of this valley. But her husband was killed in a tractor accident so she came back here. And the brothers—well, they stayed to help their father run the farm. It's too remote for outsiders to want to work here.'

They drove into a yard, parking by a group of rocks covered in lichen. At the other side of them was the same old station-wagon which the Pughs had always used to get up and down the mountainside. And sprawled in front of the house were six working sheep-dogs. The moment they saw the car they jumped to their feet, barking and wagging their tails in welcome.

Eryl looked at the wooden front door of the homestead and saw it open just enough for someone to peer through. Then she caught sight of a woman's face, which had hardly changed since she had last seen it. Suddenly filled with joy, she ran towards the house. Then she was being clasped by two warm arms and feeling as if she had never left this valley.

'Eryl, *bach*!' The words were followed by a torrent of Welsh as Ellen squeezed her even more tightly to her aproned bosom. Then there were tears and laughter and the kind of loving Eryl had forgotten in the Midlands. Pure, uncomplicated affection that made no demands. Had no false pride in it. No deception.

At last she broke away. Nodding towards Lewis, who had followed her, she said, 'Your doctor has come to see Dada.'

Ellen glanced at the man standing uncertainly by Eryl's side as if he was expecting yet another rebuff. Then she said in Welsh, 'You're going to marry him?'

Eryl felt herself blushing. 'Of course not,' she said in English. 'He's my colleague. I work with him.'

CHAPTER FIVE

WHEN Jennifer Vaughan had driven them back from Pandy, slowing down by the row of stone cottages, Eryl had not known which one was rented by Lewis. Now, as he pointed it out to her, she recognised it, remembering it as a dark and empty place where the village children had dared each other to play at their peril. It was full of ghosts, they'd said. She left the car and as Lewis pushed open an iron gate leading to a tiny front garden of weeds and wind-battered sweet williams, she laughed at the memory.

'What's so funny?' he asked.

He sounded defensive and she saw this mood as a residue from the difficult interview that he'd just had with Ellen's father. The old man had been obstinate and at one point had almost walked out of the farmhouse, refusing to listen to anything he suggested.

At last, when Lewis had given her a pleading look, Eryl had intervened as tactfully as she could, trying not to appear as if she was taking over. Speaking in fluent Welsh, she'd explained gently to the old man how essential she thought his treatment was, eventually persuading him to make certain that he really took the pills which Lewis had prescribed. Then she had asked him to think seriously about seeing a specialist.

Now she tried to reassure Lewis that there was nothing sinister in her amusement. 'It's this place,' she said, her eyes dancing. 'It takes me back to the games we played as children. Because it was empty for so long even some of the grown-ups in Dynas thought it was haunted. One day a gang of us broke in, braving the shadows, and ended up being very sorry for ourselves.'

'Why? Did you come across a ghost, after all?' He was now looking amused. Not so on edge.

'Of course,' she said, grinning back at him. 'When we were inside it came to the front door. This very door you're opening now. And we were all so scared that we just couldn't move.'

He lifted one eyebrow. 'I've heard of Celtic magic,' he said, 'but this is going too far.'

'You reckon? The consequences were horrible. Most of us got a beating. Though the aunt who'd looked after me since my mother died only gave me the lightest of taps across my hand, I remember.'

'Whatever for?'

She shrugged. 'Oh—for trespassing where we had no right to be. But most of all for being found out. You see, the ghost at the door happened to be the village policeman!'

'Really? I guess that took a lot of living down!'

Lewis ushered her into a little hall and on to a sitting-room whose only window overlooked the front garden. Furnished with a comfortable chintz-covered sofa and two matching armchairs, there was also room for two wooden chairs and a small table. A reading lamp was set on the hearth of an ancient stone fireplace filled with unlit logs.

One wall, painted with cream emulsion, was covered with shelves literally brimming with books. But the other walls were bare, their grey stone left rough—a reminder of the mountain from which they had been hewn centuries ago.

As Eryl looked around her eyes lit up with pleasure.

'It's wonderful!' she said. 'You've turned it into a real home.'

He stared at her, his dark eyes solemn. And she saw a strange kind of yearning in him. That desolation she had glimpsed before. But at last he looked away and said, 'I was lucky to find it. It's been a haven ever since. . .'

He paused and she didn't press him. She didn't want to know what was going on inside his head because the sadness she saw in him hurt her. This man shouldn't be looking vulnerable like this, she thought. It screwed her up inside and made her want to stretch out her hands to him—to touch that suntanned skin and feel the warmth of it.

And that was something that she had sworn she would not do. Not with him. Not with anyone, ever again. If she did, it would only awaken all those terrible memories of Robert. Of the way she had trusted him and believed in his love until it had been shattered. And all because he couldn't face a permanent relationship and the responsibilities that went with it.

She broke the mood by asking where he did his cooking and he seemed to drag himself back from a dark and distant place. Then a trace of amusement fleeted over his face as he said, 'In the smallest kitchen you've ever seen.'

He took her into the hall again, opening a door leading to what had once been a scullery at the back of the house. Here again he'd done his best to turn it into something manageable. A fridge stood against a rough-cast wall. There was just enough room for two wooden milking stools set beside a small table and a Welsh dresser, whose shelves were stacked with beautifully decorated crockery. This also contained drawers, presumably filled with cutlery.

Under a tiny window that gave the merest glimpse of the mountainside was a steel sink with mixer taps and a modern draining-board. Below this was a cubby-hole with saucepans on one side and a vegetable rack on the other.

'It all looks splendid,' she said. 'Did you have to do much to it before you moved in?'

'I asked the landlord to throw out the old porcelain sink and replace it with this,' he said. 'He made a fuss at first but became quite willing when I offered to pay.'

'Who owns this cottage, then?'

'You won't like it when I tell you.'

'You want to bet?' she asked. Then, seeing the same dark frown she had witnessed when they were eating supper with Trefor and the conversation had turned to the loss of the Winford-Wynne family, she said, 'Oh, no! Not Sir George Wilson!'

'Who else? Perhaps when you broke in here as a child you didn't realise you were trespassing on property owned by the Wynford-Wynnes. Apparently the old man used this place as a refuge when life in Powys Manor became too tedious, or whatever.'

Bending down to the vegetable rack, Lewis took out a lettuce and tomatoes which he ran under water before leaving them on the draining-board. Then he handed her a small, sharp-edged knife. 'Would you mind making the salad while I see to everything else?' he asked.

'Instead of singing for my supper—or rather, lunch?'

'Of course! A crusty old bachelor like me is always looking for a slave.' He took a salad bowl from the dresser, placing it near a cutting board. 'There you go,' he said. And, after opening the fridge door, he produced a dish of smoked salmon neatly covered in cling film.

'How well thought-out all this is. Being a bachelor seems to suit you,' she said and wished she hadn't spoken when she saw his face darken. 'Sorry! Forget what I said, will you? Your private life has nothing to do with me.'

'No, it hasn't,' he said grimly. 'I'm not the only man who can manage in a kitchen so please remember that. Then perhaps you'll stop handing out meaningless compliments.'

She swung round, knife in hand. 'I beg your pardon?'

He sighed. 'I don't appreciate fatuous praise. And, for heaven's sake, put that knife down before you do any real damage.'

Suddenly filled with silent fury, she turned away and banged the lettuce down onto the cutting board. She sliced it rapidly, trying to keep her hands from trembling. Afterwards she attacked the tomatoes, ending up by throwing everything into the salad bowl any which way. She didn't often lose her temper like this. But really! Fatuous praise, indeed! What she'd said had been meant sincerely.

Now giving her a rueful smile, he took the knife from her and placed it on the table. Then he held her hands and stroked the back of them gently with his thumbs.

'I'm sorry, Eryl,' he said quietly. 'I shouldn't have jumped at you like that. Just put it down to tiredness, will you?'

But that wasn't the only reason, was it? She looked into his eyes and saw real pain there. Part of her wanted to comfort him but another part of her wanted nothing to do with it.

At last she took her hands away. 'Think nothing of it,' she said briefly.

She watched him as he began to rearrange the badly mauled lettuce. When he had done this in silence, he cut thin slices of brown bread, spread them with butter and then arranged cutlery and plates on a tray with the food. Still without uttering a word, he marched off to the sitting-room with it.

She knew that he expected her to follow him but hesitated, watching him go and wondering if he would ever say anything again. Lewis had produced what could be a wonderful meal. But now she feared that it might taste no better than ashes.

For a moment Eryl considered leaving but remembered that her car was at the surgery. However silent he decided to remain, she'd have to join him. So, taking some mineral water from the fridge, she filled two glasses and took them slowly into the sitting-room.

'I thought we could use these,' she said. And found that she was speaking to his back as he stared through the window.

He swung round, still silent as he looked at her. Taking the glasses from her, he set them on the little table and said, 'I think we should start again, don't you? Bickering isn't really in my nature. Nor in yours, I'm sure. If we're to work together as Dr Dillon would wish us to we should at least try not to argue over trivial things.'

'Yes,' she said. 'We owe Trefor that. Perhaps even more now he's lying helpless in hospital. He's such a wonderful old man that we should both do our best for his sake.'

He gazed at her for a while, his eyes expressing so many different emotions that she couldn't possibly count them. At last he murmured, 'Well said, Doctor. I'm glad to see you love him as much as I do.'

He pulled out one of the dining chairs for her, then sat opposite. After that the heavy atmosphere lightened and conversation came more easily.

'I enjoyed my first morning in surgery,' she said as they began to eat.

'That's good to hear.' Looking at her seriously, he added, 'I think you're one of the bravest women I've ever met.'

She stared at him, amazed. Then at last managed to say, 'Me? Brave?'

'Yes. Don't think I didn't notice your first-day nerves. And the grit you used to overcome them. To say nothing of putting up with me when I objected to you moving your desk! Why, you even managed to keep your temper with me in the kitchen just now!'

A gentle smile lifted his lips, doing terrible things to her heart. But she tried to ignore it as she said flippantly, 'No. I just took it out on the lettuce.'

Now he was laughing, his dark eyes twinkling with genuine amusement. 'Better than attacking me with that sharp knife!'

Then, as swiftly as his laughter had come, it died. He rested his knife and fork on his plate and leant across the table, taking both her hands and squeezing them gently. 'You're like a breath of fresh air in this place, Eryl. More welcome than you'll probably ever realise.'

Reluctantly she took her hands away. 'I hope I'll manage to live up to that,' she said shakily.

'Oh, you will, I'm sure of it.' He drew in a deep breath and, looking hesitant, he said, 'There's something I think I ought to tell you. Not just because you're a colleague and I believe that knowing each other better makes working together easier but because—well, because I want to.'

She stared at him, wondering what on earth was coming now and hoping that she would be able to deal with it. 'Go on,' she murmured.

'You said just now that my private life has nothing to do with you. That's fine as far as it goes. But I think a few explanations are necessary.'

She felt a chill run over her skin. If he told her things about himself—private things—would he expect her to do the same? Reveal all that hurt she had kept buried for so long?

'What is all this?' she asked, trying to keep her voice from shaking. 'You as father confessor, with me baring my soul to you in return? You acting as psychologist, even? I didn't think you were qualified for either of those roles.' She knew she sounded flippant but she didn't know how else to deal with this.

'Heaven forbid! It's not you who should clear the air. It's me.' She waited, wishing that he wouldn't stare at her like that with those deep brown eyes looking so troubled. 'If I tell you I wasn't always a bachelor but am now a widower, would that explain why I sometimes seem preoccupied?'

She was horrified, remembering some of the shallow remarks she had made and seeing again those swift reactions intended only to defend herself. How could she have been so blind? So lacking in real understanding?

'I'm sorry,' she said. 'I should have realised.'

'How could you? Even your Celtic sixth sense wouldn't have helped because I've always kept things so close. Only Trefor knows the whole story.'

The whole story? What did he mean? 'Do you—
want to talk about it?' she asked hesitantly.

'Only to say that it's been harder to deal with than
I expected. Maybe because I was only thirty when my
wife Marian was killed in a particularly nasty road
accident four years ago. She was a doctor, too. Such a
waste of life.'

He looked bleak with remembered sorrow. But the
way he spoke when he mentioned that his wife had
been a doctor sounded almost savage. Strange. As if—
well, as if he hated the fact.

She shook her head imperceptibly, trying to clear
her thoughts. They were stupid, she told herself. Too
imaginative for comfort. Yet she could have sworn that
there was a kind of barrier there.

He sighed, suddenly looking even bleaker. Then he
said, 'Anything else—well, that's between me and my
conscience. To be kept strictly private, I'm afraid.'

She was glad. At this moment she couldn't have
borne to hear more.

'I can appreciate some of what you went through,'
she said quietly. 'Death is no stranger to me. My mother
died when I was very young and my father's sister
moved in to help bring me up. Then she died while I
was training at Guy's. Soon after that, my father died,
too. Then there was no one left. Now I'm twenty-seven
with a satisfying career so things are looking up again.'

She tried to sound cheerful for his sake. No car
accidents—no horror of sudden death haunted her like
it must haunt Lewis. Just an unsatisfactory finish to a
love affair that had started out so promisingly and had
ended with bitterness. But she'd coped with that, hadn't
she? Now, even though she sometimes felt like a widow
herself, Robert's image was at last beginning to fade.

'You never thought of marrying?' Lewis asked, as if he had read her thoughts.

'I was engaged once. But it came to nothing,' she said, gazing at him steadily as she shuttered her thoughts before she could blurt out how really terrible it had been. How Robert had not only spurned her when she'd most needed him because of what was happening to her but had been playing the field without her even suspecting.

Lewis went on looking at her for a few moments. But she couldn't bear the hidden sympathy she saw so she began to collect the empty plates.

'Shall we have some coffee?' he asked. 'I've even got some petits fours somewhere—in lieu of pudding.'

'Have we got time?'

He glanced at his watch. 'Not really. Trefor must come first, I suppose. And then there's evening surgery. So how about coffee after that? Perhaps dinner together somewhere first.'

She hesitated. 'I think I'll take a rain check on that, if you don't mind. I'll be pretty tired by then.'

'Of course! Thoughtless of me. I'd forgotten it was your first day in harness.'

She laughed, feeling more free with him since their talk. 'You make me sound like a horse!'

'Oh, no,' he said, looking at her with that sideways smile that she found so difficult to deal with. 'You're all human being. Never forget that.'

After speaking to the staff nurse in the cottage hospital and reading notes Dr Smith had left, both Eryl and Lewis saw that Trefor Dillon was at last progressing a little. The latest tests showed that his heart was healthy but there was still a query over his urine, which showed traces of sugar. Diabetes was a distinct possibility but until further tests were carried out Dr Smith's colleague at the Swanton hospital wouldn't commit himself.

When they went into the ward they found Trefor sitting up in bed and looking decidedly crotchety.

'Why is it that doctors make such bad patients?' Lewis teased, when the old man demanded his instant release.

'I'm a good patient,' he protested. 'But I'm worried about Dr Thomas here. I should be guiding her through the hoops at this stage. Not leaving her to fend for herself.'

Eryl smiled at him. 'I'm lucky,' she said, cheerfully. 'Much as I miss you, I've been managing quite well because Lewis has been most helpful. He's even given me lunch at his cottage.'

'That rapscallion actually entertained you in his own home? But that's unheard-of, child! He generally doesn't let anyone pass through the door.'

'Well, this time I did,' Lewis said. 'We had things to discuss.'

'So you're getting on all right? With each other, I mean. You'll fit in together workwise?'

'Perfectly well, thank you,' Eryl said, hoping that the present climate with Lewis would last. Then she broached the subject of Ladykins and the possibility of putting in a cat flap.

Trefor Dillon was doubtful at first but only because he thought Eryl would be taking on too much. 'Caring for five animals as well as your patients!' he exclaimed. 'How will you manage, my dear?'

Lewis snorted. 'From what I've seen of Dr Thomas she could manage a whole circus and come out unscathed.'

'Well, if you think you can do it then go ahead. It'll be good for Gwillim Pugh to make it. Give him an interest away from those eternal sheep for a change.'

Lewis then told him about the interview with Gareth Pugh and how invaluable Eryl had been. 'She not only spoke fluent Welsh to the man but she persuaded him to be reasonable over seeing a specialist.'

'So, women doctors do have their uses, after all,' Trefor said archly. 'Now perhaps you'll learn to trust them all over again.'

Eryl was astounded. This shadow of doubt hovering over women doctors seemed so strange. What on earth did Trefor mean? Was he referring to Lewis's wife?

She remembered the savage tone of his voice when he'd spoken of her. She'd dismissed it at the time, thinking that her imagination was working overtime. By rights, she should also dismiss it now. Knowing that he had been married, then widowed so tragically, was as much as she could cope with at the moment.

'Don't look so worried, my dear!' Trefor said, breaking into her dark thoughts with a smile. 'Oh, it's true that young Lewis here was once sceptical about women in medicine. Something to do with a dragon of a female professor he crossed swords with while he was training, I believe.' The old man chuckled, actually giving Eryl a wicked wink. 'But I'm sure he's getting over it. After all, his late wife was a doctor. A brilliant one, too. Isn't that right, Lewis?'

Eryl looked sharply at the man now standing rigidly by the bed and saw his dark eyes grow hard. She watched him look away as he said reluctantly, 'Yes. I'll grant you that.'

So that was what his early antagonism was all about! A narrow-minded view that could be dangerously near to bigotry. She could scarcely believe such narrow-mindedness existed in a man of Lewis's generation. Yet this didn't explain everything about his attitude, did it? There was something more, she was sure. Something to do with the kind of woman his wife had been.

As they left the ward Eryl walked silently beside him, wondering what had gone wrong with his marriage. Then she pushed the thought from her. She could do without all this! But she certainly wanted to confront him with his prejudice. So, telling herself that she needed to clear the air for the sake of her work, she said, 'Is it true, what Trefor just said?'

He stopped walking to look down at her, his face expressionless. 'About Marian being a great doctor?'

'No. I meant your mistrust of women in medicine.'

'Yes.'

'But *why*? Surely women can match men in this particular profession? I agree they wouldn't have the same strength if they pitted themselves against builders, for instance. But in *medicine*!'

Strangely, he began to laugh and she felt herself bridle. Then he said, 'I love that light of battle in your eyes.'

'Oh? Then you should just see me when I really get worked up!'

'I hope I never have to!' The smile he gave her was filled with a warm kind of amusement, as if he had enjoyed her sparring with him. Then he became serious as he admitted, 'I haven't always been easy around women doctors. But I'm learning.'

She waited for more but it didn't come so she had to be content with that.

Lewis drove her back in time for evening surgery, dropping her at the flat to collect her medical bag.

But just before she unlocked her door he called her name softly.

'Yes?' she asked, turning towards him.

'What did Ellen Pugh ask in Welsh? Before you told her I was your colleague?'

Eryl froze. There was no way she could tell him the truth. But after a moment she forced herself to speak, keeping her eyes clear and honest.

'She just asked me if you were an old friend,' she said.

And she didn't even flinch at the lie.

CHAPTER SIX

BY THE time June gave way to July Eryl was exception-
ally busy and wondered why she had ever thought this
place more peaceful than the Midland practice. One
reason for her heavy workload was Trefor Dillon's
continued absence. Not only had she acquired new
patients of her own, she had also taken on many of his.

The last time Dr Smith had examined Trefor, he'd
finally admitted that he could find no real cause for
his excessive lassitude. But, after much thought, he'd
insisted on Trefor staying in hospital for a while longer.
'Just to make certain,' he'd said.

Eryl found this remark vague and unsatisfactory but
there was little that she could do about it because,
strictly speaking, Trefor was Lewis Caswell's patient.
She had no intention of doing or saying anything that
might lead to argument, for recently Lewis had been
even more preoccupied than ever.

There were times when she suspected him of avoiding her and wondered whether this was because of
Trefor's revelations about the younger doctor's prejudice or the way he had spoken so frankly of Lewis's
wife and her brilliance as a practitioner. Anyway, she
thought that sidestepping issues that could turn out to
be contentious seemed to be wise.

Now she threw herself into her work, to the exclusion
of everything else, determined to do her best for the
old man who was still so frail. She listened to wheezy
chests, checked blood pressures, examined patients

who developed sore throats despite the mild summer weather and wrote endless prescriptions.

She also did follow-up sessions, where she met a reluctant Mr West, dragged there by his wife who was waiting anxiously to begin her hormone replacement therapy. Having suspected that he might have been browbeating his wife—or even worse, physically mal-treating her—Eryl was eventually satisfied that her anxiety was groundless. The husband turned out to be a mild little man with old-fashioned ideas, fearful, he said, of tampering with nature.

Charlie Daniels, too, was now causing his mother less heartache and Eryl's theory of a psychological slant to the boy's excessive catarrh seemed to be proved right. This pleased her for she had based it on the flimsiest of reasons.

During her medical training one of her tutors had touched on what he called 'mind over matter', citing the case of an old man who had a phobia about telephones. Whenever he made a call he was so nervous that he tightened up. He even stopped breathing for short periods. But when a normal stream of oxygen entered his body again the sinuses, which had been temporarily cut off, protested by overflowing.

Fact or fairy tale? There was nothing much written about this state and Eryl suspected that the story really belonged to folk medicine. But, being a true Celt, she had believed in it, experimented with it and come to the conclusion that it might possibly be right. For after Mrs Daniels had visited the school Charlie's teacher began actively to encourage the lad. And then, miracu-lously, his runny nose began to dry up.

Privately Eryl called this treatment 'Kidology'. But when Mrs Daniels and her now-cheerful son left the surgery, she allowed herself a moment of silent triumph.

During her work she also discovered that what some patients needed more than anything else was to talk. Pleased that they had at last accepted her, she listened—and went on listening. And because this took up so much of her time she was often the last to leave the building. Sometimes too tired even to eat properly, she managed to exist on microwave meals for one and take-aways from a restaurant that had recently opened in the village.

However, this diligence did bring her a bonus. It meant that she saw less of Lewis Caswell and this pleased her for she no longer felt ragged at the edges because of the gloom that still haunted him. Another reason she was thankful concerned the lie she had told him about Ellen Pugh. Now she didn't have to answer any more awkward questions. But, above all, she did not have to deal with his magnetic charisma, which she found increasingly upsetting.

One evening Nerys Powell invited her home for supper and at last she met Doug. 'The husband of all of six months', as Nerys had described him, was the epitome of rugged manhood. Tall, with red hair inherited from ancestors whom Dynas people called the *banditti*—those marauders who'd invaded Wales in ancient times—he was, nevertheless, a gentle giant of a man whose blue eyes never left his wife's face.

'Well? What d'you think of him?' Nerys asked, when she and Eryl were washing up while Doug shut the cows in their byre for the night.

'He's wonderful! A real angel. Kind and fun to be with, too. You're very lucky to have found such a marvellous man.'

Nerys smiled with pride. Then her face grew serious as she said, 'And you? Is there a special man in your life?'

Eryl was taken aback. She had liked the girl's frankness when she'd first met her. She had even thought of telling her about Robert Davies one day. But now her words suddenly jarred, making Eryl want to shy away.

'No, there isn't,' she said evenly. But, when Nerys stared at her as if she had suddenly turned into a stranger, she admitted, 'Well, yes, there was—once. But not any longer.'

'D'you want to talk about it?'

Did she? Not really, she supposed. It would only open up old wounds. Yet she felt she owed Nerys more than silence. The girl's offer to listen wasn't made idly, nor was it because she wanted to gossip. It was a sincere gesture of help.

At last Eryl said, 'I—I find it difficult to talk, Nerys. So I've always kept it bottled up. For years, now.'

'That's not really good, is it?' Nerys said gently. 'If you harbour things inside yourself too long they stay with you. Even grow into something that could dominate your life. Spoil it for ever, if you're not careful.'

Eryl saw a sympathy in Nerys that held no trace of maudlin sentimentality and, before she could stop herself, she told her friend things that she had never uttered to a soul until this moment. How the doctor she had loved when she was still a student had bewitched her and had talked to her of a future together that had seemed like heaven.

'So, what happened?' Nerys whispered when Eryl suddenly stopped talking.

Eryl sighed, on the edge of tears. 'This is the difficult

bit,' she said, 'to talk about. To believe, too. Even after all this time.'

As Nerys waited in silence Eryl gathered her courage. Then, in a husky voice, she said, 'We had our future all mapped out. Or at least I thought we had. But it seemed that was wishful thinking on my part. You see, he managed to get me into bed. Promising me everything in the world. And then. . . Well, after a while things went really wrong. So he just upped and left.'

'Just like that? For no reason?'

Oh, there had been a reason all right. But Eryl couldn't bring herself to speak about it. Later, perhaps, when she was feeling less fragile. But not now when the real reason for his going lay like a heavy stone deep inside her.

'You might say that,' she said quietly.

'I see,' Nerys murmured. After a long pause she said, 'I hope my listening helped. And if you ever want to talk again please remember I'm always here for you.'

'That's kind.'

'Not kind. Just something a friend should be able to do. You see, I like you, Eryl. Just as if I'd known you for years instead of such a short time.'

After that the atmosphere gradually returned to normal and stayed that way for the rest of the evening. But as she drove home Eryl found herself envying the newly married couple, longing for a life that held this sort of uncomplicated happiness. Then she told herself that she had only herself to blame for the shambles her own life had become. It was up to her to get rid of the shadows inside her, wasn't it? She should be grasping at hope and learning how to believe in herself again.

When she arrived in the courtyard she noticed that

Lewis's car was there but could see no sign of him. Then, as she got out and slammed her door, she heard footsteps. Turning, she saw him coming swiftly towards her from the main house.

'What are you doing here?' she asked. 'Is there an emergency?'

'You could say that! I've just brought Trefor home. Long before he's really fit to leave hospital. So I just slipped over to let you know.' He frowned. 'By the way, where have you been this late in the evening?'

She stiffened. Did he think he owned her, asking questions about things that didn't concern him?

'Out to supper,' she said shortly.

'Oh? Anyone interesting?'

She wanted to tell him to get lost but was too concerned over Trefor to waste time sparring with him.

'Nerys and her husband,' she said. Then she asked why he had fetched Trefor if he considered it too soon.

'Because he flatly refused to stay any longer, that's why! And can you imagine me trying to persuade him otherwise?'

She could but decided not to pursue something that might lead to a battle of words. 'So what did Dr Smith say about all this?'

'He agreed with me that Trefor should stay put. But he was just as helpless. He wasn't actually in Pandy when Trefor was making his bid for freedom but I phoned through to Swanton. When I told him Trefor was going spare he at last suggested I give in. So, after swearing to let Smith know if there's any deterioration, I checked Trefor out and drove him here.'

'But what about all those further tests? I thought Smith wanted to involve a specialist in diabetes.'

'It seems everything's OK in that department.

Trefor's borderline so, given there's no change in sugar levels, he'll be fine.'

It all seemed so casual. 'You'll be testing him regularly, I take it, and letting Smith know if there's a change. Of *any* kind?'

'Of course! Stop worrying, will you? Why don't you go and see Trefor now? Check him out for yourself? Then, afterwards, perhaps you'd like to invite me in for a drink or something.'

'I'm afraid I haven't got much in at the moment.'

'Am I to take that as a rebuff?'

She looked at him quickly, catching an expression of disappointment. He also seemed extremely weary, which touched her when she least expected it.

'No, it wasn't a rebuff! I'm sorry if I sounded sharp. You're quite welcome, of course. But there's nothing stronger than lager or coffee, I'm afraid.'

He looked closely at her in the glow shed from her outside light. She saw his face grow worried for an instant. And then he said softly, 'Perhaps it's not such a good idea, Eryl. You look worn out. You've been doing too much, haven't you?'

'No more than anyone else. You look as if you've had your fair share of slog, too.' She sighed. 'Anyway, I think we ought to meet when I've been to see Trefor. Then I can tell you what I think of him.'

'Right! I promise not to keep you long. I'd like to discuss something else with you, too.'

'Oh?' She saw him give her that wonderful smile and wished that he wouldn't do that. When it came unexpectedly like that it always managed to take her breath away and she felt too tired at the moment to cope with it.

'Don't look so worried,' he said, his voice deep and

soft. 'No more confessions, I promise! Just some work talk. There's one patient I'm worried about at the moment. I'd like to discuss him with you. Strictly professionally, of course.'

'But if he's your patient he's really nothing to do with me, is he?'

'Correction! I'm thinking of handing him over.'

'With his permission?'

'Well, er—not exactly. But he's obviously fed up with me. Behaves as if he hates my guts, in fact.'

She handed him the key to her flat, which now sported a cat flap in the front door, and told him to help himself to a drink while she visited Trefor. 'And if Ladykins and her brood are in perhaps you'd open a tin of food for them.'

'Will do, ma'am!'

Giving her a salute, he went towards his own car, opened the boot and then hastily shut it again. Afterwards she noticed him hanging about, as if he was waiting for her to leave, and she wondered vaguely what was going on. Then, telling herself not to be so nosy, she hurried away.

Mrs Reynolds was literally wringing her hands as she let Eryl into the house, pulling at her wedding ring and then flapping her arms about as if she was fending off a swarm of bees.

'What on earth are we to do, Dr Thomas?' she kept saying over and over again until Eryl quietly ordered her to stop.

At that the woman snapped her mouth shut then folded her lips into a severe line, looking as if she'd been struck. So, even more gently, Eryl said, 'It does no good to worry, you know. Dr Caswell and I will keep a close watch on Dr Dillon. If anything changes we'll get in touch with the specialist in Swanton at once.'

This seemed to calm Mrs Reynolds and just before she took Eryl into the sitting-room she actually smiled as she said, 'Thank you, Doctor. I feel he's in safe hands with you.'

So the housekeeper finally trusted her, did she? Eryl wondered how long this peace would last and then pushed the thought away. It was up to her to make certain that the truce with dear, crotchety old Martha survived.

The housekeeper went into the room with her and sat discreetly on a chair some way from the sofa where Trefor was lying, covered by a multicoloured Welsh honeycomb blanket. His eyes were closed and soft light from a standard lamp was touching his face. Eryl watched him for a moment, thinking how peaceful he looked. Then she frowned, more anxious than she wanted to admit as she noticed a waxy sheen on his cheeks.

Turning to Mrs Reynolds, she asked quietly, 'Was he as pale as this when he first arrived?'

The housekeeper nodded. 'I offered him beef tea but he refused. Didn't want to eat, either.'

'I expect he had a meal before he left Pandy.' Eryl tried to sound cheerful but inside there was a cold knot of fear that she found difficult to deal with. 'Did Dr Caswell examine him at all?'

'Oh, yes! Then he asked where you were. Said things seemed all right but that he'd be happier if you took a look at him.'

'I don't think I ought to disturb him just now. Besides, my medical bag is in the flat. All I can do is take his pulse but I don't really want to wake him.'

'Perhaps you'd just like to sit with him for a while,' Mrs Reynolds suggested. 'Let me know when you're ready to leave. I'll be in the kitchen.'

As the housekeeper left Trefor stirred. Then his eyes opened slowly as if he could hardly lift the lids. When he saw Eryl he tried to hoist himself into a sitting position but sank back again, giving her a wan smile.

'Eryl, my dear!' he said. 'What a privilege to have you visit me.'

The old-world charm was still there, she noticed. And amusement touched her as she remembered the courteous, outdated words he'd used to invite her to supper that first day. Now his eyes were shining just as they had been then. But the blue of them seemed to have faded and she felt an ache deep in her heart. She moved a little stool near to the couch, sitting on it as she took one of his hands in hers. The fingers were deathly cold and the skin felt paper-thin. Lifeless.

'Welcome home,' she said, trying to keep her smile steady. 'But should you really be here?'

'Not if Lewis had his way! He wanted me to stay in that damned place.' His voice rasped, sounding breathless. 'But I couldn't put up with it a moment longer, I tell you. I need to be here. Working again.'

She sighed, thinking that he was probably the most difficult patient she was ever likely to meet. And she just didn't know what to do. How could she tell this man that what he needed above all was rest? That, because of the unstinting care he had given his patients over the years, he was steadily burning himself out. How on earth could she suggest that it was time for him to consider retirement seriously, instead of merely lightening his workload?

'You look as if you disapprove, my dear,' he said.

'Tell me, do you know something about me that I don't?'

'Of course not. Your urine test was borderline but, apart from that, you're OK. They also say your heart isn't damaged and the X-ray showed no blockage in the arteries. I presume they gave you blood tests?'

'Yes, of course. Mainly to see if I'd had what they fondly called a concealed infarction.' He lifted one eyebrow, looking scornful. 'I prefer the good, old-fashioned term of hidden heart attack, myself.'

'Did they also test your blood for possible anaemia?'

He shrugged. 'Probably. They took enough of the stuff to keep Count Dracula happy!'

She took his wrist to check his pulse. It was faint but steady enough. Then she flipped down one lower eyelid. An absence of healthy colour worried her. It could be a temporary state caused by exhaustion, of course. But it could also be a symptom of other, some-times more sinister, conditions.

At last she got to her feet, ready to leave. 'It all seems fine to me,' she said. 'Just fine!'

'But it isn't, is it?' A shadow moved over eyes that only a moment ago had been filled with faint laughter.

'I don't really know what you mean.'

'Oh, come on, Doctor! You can't keep things from me. I know when a bedside manner conceals what the physician is really thinking.'

She frowned. She wanted to say that his imagination was running riot. But she knew that she couldn't speak with conviction so, after looking at him for a moment longer, she said, 'I think it might be a good idea to get you some further blood tests. But, of course, I'd have to speak to Lewis first. Then he'd have to contact Dr Smith about tests that have been done already.'

'What nonsense all this medical rigmarole is. Approach Smith yourself, girl! Don't leave it to Lewis.'

'But, technically speaking, you're Lewis's patient.'

'You're the one with doubts. It was your sharp eyes that saw something Dr Caswell obviously missed. So why bother him?'

'Dr Dillon! I'm surprised at you. Where is all the medical etiquette you've been taught?'

He chuckled, sounding more like his old self. 'Flown to the peak of Cader Idris with all those Celtic fairies!'

She laughed softly, pleased to see him like this. Then she said seriously, 'I don't care what you say, sir. I shall consult Lewis just the same.'

'As you like. But promise me two things, will you?'

'I might. What are they?'

'First, please don't quarrel with Lewis over diagnosis. It'll only make him difficult to work with.'

'All right. I'll try to be good. So, what's the second promise?'

He began to look weary again. 'Don't call me "sir" like that. You didn't when you first came here so don't start now. It makes me feel about a hundred.'

'Go on! You're still a young man as far as I'm concerned. An attractive one, too.'

At last he smiled at her, looking like an amused gnome, she thought. 'Stop flirting with me, will you? Save it for someone else.'

'Such as?'

'Oh, I don't know. Your private life has always been a closed book as far as I'm concerned.'

She looked sharply at him, thinking that he might be probing. But, no, he wasn't being the least intrusive. And as she looked at him she suddenly saw her father in him. Kind. Listening to her as she'd poured out her heart all those years ago. Then saying nothing more. Just holding her as if she was still a child instead of a woman who had just brought him pain. Giving her comfort by his very silence.

Suddenly filled with compassion for Trefor, she leant towards him to drop a kiss on his forehead. Something she would never have dared to do before.

'Goodnight,' she said softly. 'Let me know if there's anything you want, won't you? Anything at all.'

'There's nothing, *merchi*. I'll go up to bed now. In the morning things will seem as right as rain.'

'Like Welsh rain from the mountains?' she asked, with a sad little smile.

'Yes,' he said. 'Our rain. The soft rain of the Celts.'

Lewis was waiting for her in her sitting-room, sprawled in one of the armchairs with the family of cats padding all over him. She laughed softly, unable to fit this image into the picture of stern efficiency that he usually presented.

Startled, he stood up and the cats scattered, running into the kitchen.

'So! What's so amusing?'

This remark was becoming quite a habit, she thought. A cliché, uttered defensively before he waited impatiently for an answer. 'The cats look so funny,' she said. 'They seem to have taken you over.'

He relaxed visibly. 'What d'you expect with someone who's always admired all the feline clan? Yes, even leopards and lynx! I love their effortless, almost boneless, walk. The mystery that surrounds them and the caring way the females bring up their families. To say nothing of the love domestic cats offer to humans, without ever losing their independence.'

'Quite a speech!' she said. Then, looking at him through narrowed eyes, she wondered how many more surprises he harboured. Not only was he a man who could be stern, efficient and hard on himself, he could also be positively *sloppy* over animals.

'I've fed them, as you asked,' he said. 'But I didn't help myself to a drink. Thought I'd wait for you.'

'Beer or coffee?' she asked.

'Oh, coffee, please. I've got to drive myself home, remember.'

She slipped into the kitchen, then heard him following her. Turning round, she suddenly found him much too close for comfort. There was also a strange, almost excited, expression in the depth of his eyes that pulled at her so she stepped away. Filling the percolator at the sink, she spooned coffee into the container, put the jug on the stove and lit the gas.

'Why don't you make yourself comfortable in the sitting-room while I do this?' she suggested. 'You must have had quite a day.'

'I'm fine here, thank you. Besides, I wanted to see how long it'd be before you noticed this.'

Puzzled, she turned back to him and then saw him pointing to the far end of the room which lay in shadow. There, tucked cosily into a corner, was a round flat basket lined with a soft blanket. And lying in it was Ladykins, purring loudly as she suckled her family.

Was this why he had returned to his car and hung about waiting for her to leave?

'You—you brought this?'

'No. I *bought* it. Specially for the new family.'

'You must be mad!'

'Maybe. But when I knew for sure you were serious about taking the cats in and then thought how chilly they'd be when autumn comes I felt this was the least I could do. So welcome to one of Old Man Lloyd's best products!'

'How kind,' she said. And whether it was the way that his caring had touched her or because she was so desperately tired she didn't know. Whatever caused it, she felt her eyes filling with tears and had to look away from him.

'Hey! What is all this?' he asked, holding her arms and pulling her towards him. 'Are you upset because of Trefor?'

'No, it's nothing like that.' She sniffed, then found a white handkerchief being pushed gently into one hand and wiped her face, ashamed that he should see her like this. 'It's—well, your kindness, I suppose. I didn't expect it and I'm certain I don't deserve it. Thank you for thinking of Ladykins like that.'

The percolator began to bubble and she moved away from him. But a moment later his hands were on her arms again and he was turning her to face him. She looked up at him but when tears threatened again she shifted her gaze.

'Please, Eryl!' he said. 'Please, please look at me. There's something else, isn't there? Something that's weighing you down. That you want to talk about but can't. Oh, my dear. Don't shut yourself away like this.'

Feeling desperate, she said, 'Isn't it time we talked about Trefor? And that patient you want to hand over to me?'

'All in good time. You're the one who's important now. So tell me what makes you cry like this.'

Unable to utter a word, she felt his hands slacken but he didn't let her go. Then his fingers moved to her face and were touching her cheeks, tracing a pattern over each curve until they reached her chin. She found that she couldn't move; couldn't break the spell that was holding her.

After a while his lips traced the same pattern, moving over her skin with a touch as soft as cobwebs. Then his tongue stretched out to the wetness that was still beneath her eyes and he licked away the salt tears.

Like Ladykins grooming her kittens, she thought crazily and gave herself up to the warmth of his velvet touch.

Soon his arms were around her, pressing her body close to his. She didn't quite know how this had happened. She only knew that a few moments ago she hadn't wanted it to. But now she was fearful that it might stop. His lips, still damp and salt from touching her tears, moved slowly over her own. She could feel the heat of his rapid breath. Smell the scent of him that was all man. And she could sense silent questions in those dark eyes as they skimmed her own.

Then his eyes closed as his mouth pressed harder against hers, his tongue prising her lips open and seeking the warmth inside her mouth. And she was lost in a whirlpool of sensation. It ran through her like a torrent, touching all those secret places in her that she thought had been numbed for ever.

As she felt his heart beating against hers she closed her own eyes and gave herself up to a fire that she'd thought no longer existed in her. There seemed to be a vast world of emotion encompassing them. As if this was meant to be. As if his soul was meeting hers.

Then suddenly he drew back and she cried out, feeling pain because he was no longer touching her. And as her eyes flew open she saw a shadow pass over his and witnessed a kind of agony in them.

'What is it?' she whispered.

He pushed her gently away from him, regret showing on every inch of his face. 'I'm sorry,' he said. 'I shouldn't be kissing you like this. I—I can't. . .'

'Why not? Is it so wrong of us?'

'No. Not wrong. But it's not right, either. There's something—you just don't know.'

'To do with your wife?'

'In a way,' he said, his voice strangely flat. 'But it's also about me. It's difficult to explain but it means I can never get involved. I didn't mean to lead you on like this so please forgive me.'

He meant that he was still in love with his wife, didn't he? The woman who had died was still with him.

He hadn't struck her but it felt as if he had. In that instant she came to her senses.

Fool! Fool! The silent words rang in her ears as if she had spoken them aloud. What was she thinking of—breaking down the barrier of safety she had held inside herself for so long?

At last, forcing a little smile and trying to control a shake in her voice, she said, 'I'm sorry, too. This shouldn't have happened. So shall we take the coffee into the sitting-room? Begin the work discussion you suggested?'

The look on his face was grim. 'Yes,' he said, sounding infinitely weary. 'Let's do that thing.'

As she carried the tray of coffee into the sitting-room Eryl knew that they would never get down to work. The atmosphere was too fraught with tension because of what had happened between them. The cruelty of Lewis's rejection bit into her, bringing back a sharp memory of the pain that she'd suffered with Robert.

And for this she thought she would never be able to forgive him.

She poured out the coffee in silence. Then, scarcely able to glance at him as he sat awkwardly on the edge of an easy chair, she handed him a cup.

At last he said, 'I was wrong, Eryl. Now isn't the right time to talk about patients. Tomorrow, perhaps.' And, after hurriedly drinking only half his coffee, he clashed the cup down into the saucer and moved towards the door.

His back was stiff—excluding her. She couldn't see his face but imagined that it held the same shuttered expression she had seen when they were in the kitchen. Then, in no time at all, he was down the stairs, shouting 'Goodnight!' and slamming the front door behind him as he went into the courtyard.

She stood on the landing, then switched off the outside light as she heard him driving away. And all the time something dark and hollow began to grow inside her. Its very emptiness seemed to expand, taking away her breath as she fought against tears.

'Damn the man!' she said aloud. Over and over again she heard her voice intoning the senseless words until they took on the obsessional pattern of sound uttered by some insane patient.

Working with him, she'd thought that she had at last begun to understand him and had found a kind of camaraderie growing between them. Now she realised that she didn't know him at all. Neither did she know herself any longer. Her own reactions to his touch filled her with despair. Not only had she been determined to resist the charm that tempted her, now she was actually regretting his leaving.

At last she forced herself to go to the bathroom,

where she washed all sign of tears from her face. Pulling on the T-shirt she slept in, she took the dirty coffee-cups to the kitchen. Tonight she had no strength to deal with them so she left them in the sink. Ladykins and her kittens were settled in Lewis's basket and she watched their soft bodies moving gently as they breathed. So cosy, she thought. So uncomplicated. Just living the life they were meant to live.

Reluctantly she left them, little balls of fluff snuggled against each other for comfort. Then she went to bed, hoping for sleep. But it refused to come until she saw dawn breaking over the mountains.

CHAPTER SEVEN

THE next few days were so busy that Eryl had no time to think of anything apart from work. Thankfully, these days Lewis seemed to avoid her and whenever she saw him she stepped briskly out of his way. But all the time she gradually sank deeper into herself. Now, shunning the usual chit-chat that she had once enjoyed with the women in Reception, she concentrated all her energy on dealing with patients.

However, she managed to make time for Trefor, slipping across to the main house to visit him every day. As she went in she always gave Mrs Reynolds a bright smile and tried to keep it on her face during the short time that she spent with the old doctor.

He seemed to be making some real progress now. The blood tests for anaemia revealed nothing sinister so, after prescribing some extra-strong iron pills for him, Lewis told him to continue to take things easy and everyone put his lethargy down to advancing years.

'What about a little holiday?' Eryl suggested.

'My life is one long holiday these days! All I need is to see you from time to time.' He smiled at her, flirting, as he added, 'You, my dear, are a real POG.'

She laughed. 'I thought my Welsh was near perfect. But I don't know that word. What on earth does it mean?'

'It's English, *merchi*! Initials meaning a Power Of Good.'

'Oh—*you*!' She took his hand and squeezed it.

'I never had any children,' he said. 'But if I'd been fortunate enough to father a daughter she'd be just like you, Eryl.'

Pleased because he'd made her feel wanted, she brushed his cheek with her lips. 'Thank you for that,' she said. 'Now I must go. Promise me you'll continue with the rest treatment. No dancing about the place with Mrs Reynolds, now!'

She never stayed long. She didn't dare in case his sharp eyes spotted the emptiness inside her. If he found her hurried departures strange he said nothing. And she hoped that he would blame her full workload for it.

But her behaviour did not go unnoticed elsewhere. One day she caught the two receptionists giving her strange looks and when at last Betty Williams enquired sharply if she was unwell she tried to laugh it off.

'Never felt better!' she said. 'Why d'you ask?'

Glynis Jones elbowed Betty aside, a sympathetic smile on her motherly face that almost flayed Eryl. She said, 'We're not being nosy, love. But you look so— lost, somehow. Is it because of Dr Dillon?'

Eryl grasped at this explanation with relief. 'Yes, I suppose it must be. I always think worry is the very devil. It pulls you down quicker than anything,' she said.

But when Nerys saw her the next day after morning surgery she went straight to the heart of things in that direct way of hers. 'What's with the pale face?' she asked. 'Want to talk some more?'

Eryl panicked. 'Sorry! But I'm rather busy right now.'

'Thought your last patient had left.'

'I've got visits to do. And a heap of paperwork.'

At that moment Lewis came out of the treatment

room, asking crossly how it was that they all seemed
to have time to gossip.

Eryl saw Glynis raise surprised eyebrows before she
picked up a sheaf of papers waiting for her attention.
Then Nerys gave everyone a mirthless smile and hurried off. As if she, too, feared the wrath now burning
in Lewis Caswell's eyes.

Looking directly at Eryl for the first time in ages, he
said, 'I'd like you to come to my surgery. We have
things to discuss.'

'Sorry! I'm frantically busy. Later, perhaps?'

'No, not later. Now. This very moment.'

She wanted to refuse but, seeing fire kindling in
him, she did as he asked before he could explode and
followed him to his room. She hoped that this interview
would be about the patient he wanted her to take over.
If it turned out to be more personal she was damned if
she would stay! At last, sitting nervously in a chair
opposite him as he went behind his desk, she waited
for him to begin. Please, oh please, talk work! she
said silently. And when he did just that, with his usual
impersonal efficiency, she began to breathe more easily
and forced herself to look at him.

The patient whom he wanted to hand over was David
Morland, who lived in a caravan in the mountains.
'He's an eccentric of thirty-five but looks all of fifty,'
Lewis said. 'People believe he's a left-over from a
group of travellers who stayed in this area some
time ago.'

'Have you squared this move with him?'

'I tried but he's obstinate. I thought you might like
to talk to him. He'll probably open up to you because
you're a woman.'

What was this? Lewis at last overcoming his prejudice about women doctors? Or using her as bait dangled in front of a mendicant?

'So why d'you want to get rid of him?' she asked.

'You name it!' Lewis shrugged, looking so hopeless that she suddenly wanted to touch him. She even felt her fingers moving so she clamped her hands together, keeping them firmly in her lap.

'What's wrong with him?'

'Would you believe—indigestion?'

She was tempted to laugh but managed to stop herself when she saw his jaw tighten and his eyes take on a steely look. He was challenging her, she thought. Egging her on to argue, when the last thing she needed was to cross swords with him. Especially after that last battle of emotions.

She stood up. 'Well, I suppose I'd better go and see him. Can I have your notes on him to read before I leave?'

'Certainly. But you won't be going alone.'

'Why ever not?'

'Because I say so. I shall be coming with you.'

This was getting ridiculous. First offering her as an inducement to the mystery man and now acting like a Victorian chaperon. Why, oh, why did everything have to be so complicated around Lewis?

'So, when do you propose we should go?'

'Now.'

'But I already have visits planned for this afternoon.'

'Do them later. Get Glynis to phone your patients for you. Put them off till tomorrow if necessary. This is more important.'

She sighed with frustration. 'I'm just not ready for this! How do you expect me to deal with a man I've never met without first reading his medical history?'

'Just stop blethering, Eryl! You sound hysterical.'

How dared he? Talking to her as if she was a child who needed a good hard smack! Where was the gentleness that he'd shown only a short while ago? The loving that he'd displayed? Had it all been erased from his mind?

Of course it had. He'd made sure of it, hadn't he? Forgetting the incident immediately after it had happened. Then leaving her abruptly with no real explanation of his irrational behaviour.

But you wanted him to go!

The truth of this pulled at her and she stifled her thoughts before she could make a fool of herself again. She even smothered a desire to hit back at him.

'Sorry!' she said, evenly. 'Perhaps you can fill me in with information as we go to this caravan.'

'OK!' he said. 'Shall we take my car?'

'If you like. You probably know the way better than I do.'

They went to the courtyard and he opened the passenger door of his car for her, waiting for her to settle herself before he eased himself into the driving seat. Then he thrust his hand into the glove box, producing a packet of ready-prepared egg and cress sandwiches which he offered to share with her.

'You think of everything, don't you?' she said, with a coolness she was far from feeling.

'I try. We have lonely places in Scotland, too, you know. There no one ever travels far without taking some form of food. Just in case there's a breakdown.'

They drove along the main road, then turned into a mountain track new to Eryl. On and on they went until they were climbing even higher—into a lonely spot she thought too isolated for anyone to live in.

'If this man wants the outdoor life why doesn't he rent one of the holiday caravans on the other side of the valley?' she asked. 'At least he'd get hot water there and a camping shop.'

'Because he's a recluse, that's why. It beats me how he ever got round to registering with our practice in the first place.'

'So what is he, exactly? And what does he do with his time, tucked away up here?'

'By his appearance you'd think he had no education. But he has. Holds a doctorate in literature. Used to be a university lecturer, I'm told. But gave it all up to come here.'

'So, what does he do for a living?'

'Freelance work. He's a publisher's reader.'

'What! How on earth does he manage? Posting off manuscripts and so on.'

'Ask him. He'll probably tell you lots of things he just can't bring himself to tell me.'

He paused and she looked at him, seeing a bleakness in his face that she suddenly found she couldn't bear. At last she said, 'Is he really that bad with you?'

He shrugged. 'My own fault, I suppose. I lost patience with him. Then he just shut himself off from me.'

He stopped the car at the bottom of a rutted path leading to a real Romany van. She expected to see a horse nearby, cropping the grass. But instead there was an old BMW that had long since ceased to be the status symbol it once was.

As they got out of the car Eryl lifted her face to the mountain wind. Far above her she could see a pair of buzzards gliding slowly across the sky on thermal streams. She watched them soaring and dipping with infinite grace and at last felt her spirit lifting with their flight. Then she stood quite still, listening. Apart from the trilling of a lark as it rose far into the sky and the gentle shushing of wind that was lifting the sedge at the side of the track, there was only silence.

'I envy this man,' she said.

When Lewis didn't reply she turned to look at him and what she saw disturbed her even more than his bleakness had. His gaze was on her face, probing, as if he was trying to reach her inner thoughts. There was a softness there, too. And a strange mixture of other emotions that she couldn't hope to understand.

At last he said quietly, 'You love this place, don't you? It's more than just scenery to you. So, what is it that makes you look like that? As if you were a part of these mountains?'

She gave a little, breathless laugh. 'I suppose I really am a part of them. Always have been, even though I left them for so long.'

He studied her in silence for a moment longer. Then he said, 'If you envy David Morland I think I envy you more.'

'What an extraordinary thing to say! The mountains belong to us all.'

He shrugged. 'For me it's not the same. I fear them. I see danger in them because I know the menace they can become if they're not treated with respect.'

From the corner of her eyes Eryl saw a movement and looked towards the caravan. A man wearing jeans and a ragged pullover was leaning against the open door. Fair hair straggled to his shoulders and his thin face was strained and almost colourless.

Eryl wondered if he always looked like this. Even at this distance and without examining him he seemed to her like a typical candidate for a heart attack. Or even stomach ulcers, she thought and the indigestion Lewis had mentioned now took on new meaning.

After watching them closely the man frowned. He obviously saw them as unwelcome intruders.

'We'd better move on,' she said. 'We've been spotted.'

They walked farther up the track, avoiding a handful of sheep nibbling tufts of coarse grass, and stopped a short way from the man.

'Hi, there!' Eryl meant to sound relaxed and friendly but as the man went on staring in silence she faltered.

Thankfully Lewis took over, introducing her properly.

The man's frown turned into a dark scowl as his bright blue eyes moved slowly from Lewis's face to her own. 'Is this a professional visit?' he asked. 'I don't remember asking you to come.'

'No, you didn't,' Lewis said easily. 'But that's no reason why we shouldn't call, is it?'

'If it's just a social thing then I have to tell you I'm much too busy to entertain. So I'll say goodbye to you.'

His voice was cultured, making a mockery of his tramp-like appearance. It was also strong, with more than just a hint of anger in it. Eryl knew that she would think twice before crossing him and was suddenly grateful that Lewis was here. When they showed no sign of leaving the man stepped inside the van and slammed the door shut after him. This incensed Lewis and he rushed at the door, banging on it loudly.

'Will you kindly show a few manners!' he shouted. 'For God's sake, I only want you to meet our new doctor.'

No wonder the man hated Lewis's guts, as he put it.

If this was the way the pair of them carried on then she wouldn't be surprised if one day they actually came to blows. And what would happen to the Dynas surgery then? She could picture court cases and medical tribunals, to say nothing of the pain it would cause Trefor Dillon. Now angered herself, she felt a stiffening of her courage and marched up to the closed door.

After rapping on it sharply, she said, 'Mr Morland! Never in my life have I met such rudeness. If it's your intention to continue in this—this uncouth way then the only thing left to us will be. . .'

She didn't finish for at that moment he opened the door and thrust his head through. She stepped back sharply before his face could collide with hers and found herself staring into blue eyes that were now bright with humour.

'And what is the only thing left to you?' he enquired, sounding sardonic.

If he expected her to waver he would be disappointed, she thought. So, after giving him a scathing glare, she steeled herself to say, 'We are perfectly at liberty to strike your name from our lists, you know. If you object to that you can always lodge a complaint with the Regional Health Authority, of course. But it would be your word against ours and I doubt if they'd think it worth the trouble to give you even a preliminary hearing.'

She hoped that this would flatten him. But it didn't, although it certainly changed him. The disagreeable expression was instantly wiped from his face and replaced by a wide smile.

'Well done, Doctor,' he said, his eyes now skimming over her so intimately that she felt herself flush. 'Not only beautiful, I see, but clever, too. And brave. Oh yes, so very brave.'

'So! The dreadful David Morland is actually prepared to change doctors,' Lewis said as they drove down the mountain again. 'I told you your being there would make it work, didn't I?'

Eryl smiled with amusement. 'What d'you think finally turned the tables? Your brand of shouting or mine?'

'Neither. Just the sight of you was enough. I'm told he has quite a reputation with women.'

'So that means you'll always be offering yourself as a chaperon when I come here, does it?'

'You should be so lucky! What makes you think I want to chaperon you?'

What, indeed?

'So your insistence on coming with me today was. . .'

'A safety measure. Mainly for myself, I must confess. I knew if you spoke to him he'd listen. He wouldn't dare to raise his fists like he did last time.'

This riled her. 'What right have you got to put me in that sort of danger?'

He moved his gaze from the track for a moment and she saw his eyes twinkling, which made her even angrier. Then he said quietly, 'You were never in any danger, Eryl.'

'How d'you make that out?'

He chuckled softly. 'Whatever else the man may be he's the perfect gentleman where women are concerned. Even if he fancies them.'

They reached the main road, driving towards the surgery, but after only a short distance Lewis turned off to another track that was parallel to the one they had just left.

'Where are we going now? I need to get back to the surgery.' Eryl's voice was sharp with annoyance.

He turned his head briefly, a taunting smile hovering on his lips. 'Oh, don't worry! I'm not about to lose you in the mountains. We're going a new way to the Pughs' farm to see how the old man's getting on with the drugs I prescribed. And to have another go at him about seeing a specialist. Besides, it'll give you a chance to see your friend Ellen, too.'

Eryl quietened down, finding this idea attractive even though it meant that she'd have to shelve her paperwork for longer. 'Hmm. We could also beg a cup of tea,' she said, and at last felt her spirits lifting.

Although the door was wide open the Pughs' farmhouse seemed to be deserted. There was no sign of the station-wagon but that was not unusual, of course. One or other of the men often took it to the village to buy provisions.

What did seem unusual was the quietness of the place. And the way four of the six working sheepdogs lay dozing in the yard, scarcely raising their heads as they heard Eryl and Lewis leave the car. They were usually so friendly, jumping up and wagging their tails whenever anyone came into the yard. But these animals seemed thoroughly dejected, which Eryl found more than just strange. It was also frightening.

'And where are the other two?' she asked.

'The other two what?'

'Dogs. There are six of them, though only two at a time work together.'

'That's where they'll be, then. Out on the mountain with old Pugh and his sons,' Lewis said.

'At this late hour? By now they're usually rounded up, protected by dry stone walls and wire fences or whatever.' She shivered suddenly. 'I don't like this. Something must have happened.'

'Why don't we try the house before we jump to conclusions?' Lewis suggested reasonably.

He followed Eryl through the open door and they walked around the place, pacing the stone-flagged floors and even going upstairs to the bedrooms. The house was completely empty.

Yet the table laid in the kitchen looked ready for a family meal with cups, saucers and plates arranged on a snowy cloth. There were also freshly cut slices of bread and butter heaped on a glass dish, with a pot of strawberry jam next to it. And, hanging from a chain over a peat fire in the black leaded grate, a large kettle was puffing with steam. Ready to be used, Eryl thought. As if the Pughs had merely popped out for a short while.

But this was nonsense. 'For as long as I've known them the house has never been left empty like this,' she said. 'Something dreadful must have happened.'

They returned to the yard where the dogs were still stretched out listlessly.

And then they heard it. A weird sound of an animal keening, which was followed by hysterical barking. Immediately the four animals in the yard stood up and walked slowly towards the sound, their tails curled between their legs.

'Just look at that!' Eryl said. 'They know, even if we don't. What's more, they're afraid.'

They followed the dogs away from the house, past the dairy and the cowshed. They skirted an area cordoned off with fencing where the Pughs did their shearing and went on to a sunken sheep dip, eventually pausing by a gate that led to a sloping field. Here hay was grown for winter fodder but it had now been harvested, leaving only patches of stubble.

Because all the work was done, Eryl thought that no one would be here. But at the far end of the field she saw what looked like a pile of coats. And beside it, lying flat on the ground, were the two missing dogs.

Sensing the four animals that had walked so reluctantly from the yard, the dogs in the field suddenly lifted their heads and raised their voices—sounding so like wolves that an involuntary shiver ran over Eryl's skin.

Then she saw two people she hadn't noticed before kneeling beside the dogs so she shouted in Welsh, 'What's happened?'

One of the people was Gwillim, who stood up and shouted back. Eryl immediately translated for Lewis. 'It's old Gareth,' she said. 'He's collapsed.'

They sprinted across the field and found Mrs Pugh crouched beside her husband, whose top half was covered with the coats they had seen. His left foot was lodged firmly in a crack between two boulders and his face was pale, screwed up with pain. Then Eryl noticed a gash that was still bleeding on one hand.

Lewis took in the picture immediately, slackening the man's laces and opening the top of his boot as far as he could. But there was no way that he could pull the foot free so he examined as much of it as he could see. When he touched the ankle Gareth winced so he quickly withdrew his hand.

'How is it?' Eryl murmured as she knelt beside him.

'Not good. But he's obviously in such pain I daren't probe too much. I can't really tell if there's a break or not.' He smiled down into Gareth's pale face and said slowly and clearly, 'I'll give you something to ease that pain. Then we'll decide what to do for you.'

He told Eryl to stay with Gareth while he fetched his medical bag from the car and just before he left he asked Gwillim where the rest of the family was.

'Llew's taken Ellen in the station-wagon to a neighbour who has a phone,' Gwillim replied in English. 'She'll send for an ambulance but I think it'll be too hard to get it all the way up here.'

'Don't you have a phone yourselves?' Lewis sounded incredulous.

'No. Dada doesn't like them.'

Lewis gave Eryl a look of exasperation, then went to his car. Meanwhile Eryl did what she could to make the old man more comfortable, folding one of the coats beneath his head and binding his hand with a clean white scarf Mrs Pugh offered.

'There was a rogue dog, trying to kill our sheep,' the woman said in Welsh, sounding near to despair. 'Gareth chased after it but it turned on him and bit his hand. He went after it again with the shepherd's crook he always takes everywhere but it disappeared. On his way back he slipped and this—terrible thing happened.'

Eryl squeezed Mrs Pugh's shoulders, trying to calm her. Then she asked, 'Has Gareth had a tetanus jab lately?'

'I can't remember. Is it important?'

'Of course it is. You know that only too well, don't you? But not to worry. We'll see about that when we get his leg free,' she said.

But how they were going to remove the foot from its prison of stone Eryl didn't know and felt a wave of despair deep inside her which she tried not to show.

When Lewis came back she told him about the rogue dog and the doubt about Gareth's tetanus update.

'Right! We'll do something about that as soon as possible,' he said. 'But for now we must concentrate on controlling his pain.'

He produced a syringe, drew off a weak solution of morphine from one of the capsules he always carried for emergencies, and asked Eryl to roll back the man's sleeve.

'Hold on, Mr Pugh,' he said, giving the man a gentle smile as he spurted air from the syringe. 'You'll feel a little scratch at first but after a while the pain in your foot should ease.'

When he had finished injecting the fluid Eryl said quietly, 'How on earth are we going to free that foot? It seems to be stuck fast.'

Lewis narrowed his eyes as he looked at Gareth lying there with such patience, then walked round the smaller of the boulders that had trapped him. Assessing its position and weight, Eryl thought, still wondering what he could possibly do about it.

At last he gave Eryl a confident smile that steadied her. 'It's easy,' he said. 'Gwillim and I will dig him out.'

Understanding exactly what was wanted of him, the young man hurried to the yard and came back with two spades. Lewis threw off his jacket and rolled up his shirt sleeves, then he and Gwillim began to dig round the smaller of the boulders. Eryl watched them both straining, each man pitching as deep as the hard ground would allow and pausing only to rest their backs. With every thrust they made sweat ran down their faces and she could hear their breath growing harsher with each movement.

She hadn't realised that Lewis was so strong and felt herself growing almost hypnotised by muscles that rippled in his bare arms, stretching to their limit and then relaxing, ready for the next strong thrust. He moved so easily, with a rhythm that seemed to come naturally to him. Almost as if he had been trained as a labourer instead of a doctor.

Then she remembered that he had been in Africa with the World Health Organisation and supposed that he was used to working under dire conditions, perhaps even in one of the many war zones that kept occurring in that strife-ridden continent. But he hadn't talked about it and she had never probed.

Although both men were digging hard, Eryl thought that they could never shift a boulder that had been buried like that for centuries. But at last she saw it move. Just a little at first but enough to give them leverage. Gwillim dropped his spade and thrust his bare hands down the deep hole they had made, then scrabbled beneath the stone until he was able to heave the rock on its side while Lewis pushed it away from Gareth's foot.

'Thank God!' Mrs Pugh said as she watched Lewis pull the man's foot gently from his boot.

Eryl encircled the woman's shoulders with her arm again. 'Come to the house with me now,' she said. 'You need a cup of strong tea.'

'No! I'll stay where I am. I must be the one to tell the ambulance men they're not needed now.'

'What are you talking about?' Eryl asked quietly.

'My Gwillim and the doctor got Gareth out, didn't they? So the other men won't have any digging to do.'

Eryl sought Lewis with eyes that were now showing

the despair that she had tried to conceal. He caught her glance and asked, 'Is something wrong?'

'Yes,' she said quietly and told him what the woman intended to do about the ambulance.

'Not to worry,' he said softly. Facing Mrs Pugh with the same gentle smile that he had given Gareth, he said, 'We still need the ambulance, my dear. To take your husband to hospital. For X-rays and so on and possibly to keep him in for a while after the shock he's just had.'

'Hospital?' The woman looked stricken and Eryl realised, too late, how the mere mention of such a word would fill her with dread.

Mrs Pugh belonged to a generation who thought of hospitals as places where people died. The fact that Gareth Pugh had once been to Swanton when he'd been gored by that bull years ago and had returned home alive and well after treatment cut no ice with her. As far as she was concerned he'd just been lucky that time. It didn't matter what anyone said. To her all hospitals were to be feared.

Eryl saw Lewis frown and stepped in quickly before he could make matters worse. 'Just leave this to me,' she said quietly. 'After a spot of tea and gentle talk everything will go smoothly. You'll see.'

CHAPTER EIGHT

ERYL led Mrs Pugh away, still protesting. Then she sat her down at the kitchen table.

'The tea is in that canister on the mantelpiece,' Mrs Pugh said. Then she laughed softly as she added, 'Oh, of course! You'll know where to find it. Very little has changed since you lived in Dynas, my dear.'

She was right, even down to the brand of tea they used. Nothing as modern as teabags had ever entered this house. Even the silver strainer was the same, polished by Ellen until it sparkled.

Eryl tipped the large swinging kettle, pouring a little water into a brown earthenware pot to heat it. After throwing the water away in the scullery sink she spooned a liberal amount of leaves into the pot, filled it with boiling water and set it on the hob to mash.

'So! You haven't forgotten how strong we like our tea here, then,' the old lady said, still looking pale with shock but now managing to smile a little.

'No, I haven't. But you seem to have forgotten how I always told you a brew as thick as this was bad for you.'

Mrs Pugh shrugged. 'Each to their own devil, I say. At least no one in my house has ever touched that other devil, alcohol.'

Although she was serious about what she said the old lady was smiling with the kind of impish fun that Eryl remembered well. It made the subject of hospitals easier to broach and after they had sat silently drinking

111

their tea for a while she began to talk about how good
the hospital in Swanton was.

'But I don't want my Gareth to go there. He needs
me with him.' Mrs Pugh sighed, looking hopeless. 'It's
not like that time long ago when we were both younger.
I could get in to see him every day then, *merchi*. But
now I really don't think I could stand the journey.'

Was this the only obstacle holding her back? If so,
then surely something could be done. Eryl didn't know
the workings of this particular hospital but she had
come across similar places in the Midlands where
accommodation was sometimes provided for the next
of kin if there were difficulties about visiting. She knew
this mainly concerned mothers of young children but
she didn't see why it could not also apply to the elderly.

Plunging in without a second thought, she said, 'But
you wouldn't have to travel there every day. I'm sure
the hospital would find a room for you.'

She knew that suggesting it was risky but just didn't
care. Especially when she saw pleasure suddenly light-
ing up the woman's eyes. Now it was up to her to make
all this come true.

'If I go I'll need to take some night things, won't I?'
Mrs Pugh sounded eager. 'Would you help me to pack,
Eryl? You know where the cases are so please get what
I need from my bedroom, will you?'

'Of course. But before you actually leave you must
wait for me to make the arrangements. You realise that,
don't you?'

'Yes, of course. But it's better to be ready, isn't it?'

Eryl nodded, bounding upstairs to pack what she
thought Mrs Pugh would need into a small weekend
case and hurrying down just as the ambulance arrived.
Ellen and Llew had driven in front of it, guiding the

way from their neighbour's house to their own homestead. But it could get no farther than the yard so two
men carried a stretcher to the field. When Eryl looked
through the window and saw them returning with
Gareth she asked Mrs Pugh if she would like to see her
husband off.

'No, my dear. I'll stay here for a while. After all I'll
be seeing him later, won't I? When I go to stay.'

The old lady looked so frail that Eryl felt a lump
rising in her throat and at that moment became more
determined than ever to get her a visitor's bed in
Swanton. She slipped out to wish Gareth Pugh good
luck and found Lewis giving written instructions about
his case to the ambulance men, telling them to hand
them over as soon as they got to the hospital.

'Now I suppose I'd better face an irate Mrs Pugh,'
he said as the men drove off and he followed Eryl back
to the house.

'Not at all,' she said. 'Come and see for yourself.'

Amazed when he found Mrs Pugh now in agreement,
he took Eryl aside to ask how she had managed to
persuade her.

'Bribery,' she said, chuckling. 'I told her she'd be
welcome to stay in Swanton for as long as she liked.
That the authorities would find her a bed.'

His amazement turned to thunder. 'You did *what*?'
he muttered, a dangerous light in his eyes. 'But they
just don't do that sort of thing.'

'You've obviously heard of mother and sick
child units?'

'Of course, but they're rare in this area.' He then
noticed the small case Eryl had packed for the woman
and stiffened. 'And you can just get rid of that thing
for a start,' he snapped.

'Please keep your voice down, Dr Caswell,' Eryl said severely. 'If you don't you'll alarm my patient.'

'*Your* patient? What the devil d'you mean?'

'You think they won't accommodate Mrs Pugh? Well, we'll just have to see about that, won't we? If they refuse I'll ask them to admit her as a patient. After all the trauma of this afternoon I consider she needs hospital bed rest.'

His face grew dark and he turned away, moving towards the door.

'Where do you think you're going?' she asked.

As he turned back to her she flinched at the fury she saw burning in him. 'I'm about to get into my car. Then I'm going to follow the ambulance to hospital,' he said, glowering at her and speaking slowly as if he was dealing with a child of low intelligence.

'You're leaving me here?'

'Of course. I'm sure Llew will drive you to your flat if you ask him nicely. You'll be just in time for evening surgery.'

She glanced at her watch. It was almost six o'clock. 'So, what about your own surgery?' she asked.

'I'll phone through to Betty Williams or whoever's on duty and tell her to hold my patients back. Of course if I'm very late you could see them yourself.'

With that he went through the open door and Eryl tried to smile for Mrs Pugh's sake, even though she was seething. Ellen, who had come in to be with her mother and had heard most of this turgid conversation, stared at Eryl with disbelief.

'Is Dr Caswell often like that?' she asked as Lewis disappeared.

Eryl suddenly felt as if a heavy weight were hanging from her heart and found it difficult to breathe for a moment. At last she said, 'Not often, but he does have his moments.'

'But why? He seems such a nice young man.'

Eryl shrugged. 'I—think he may have problems. Personal ones he doesn't want people to know about.'

'Like you did? When you left Dynas?'

Eryl turned to Ellen, her eyes suddenly stinging. 'But mine weren't exactly secret, were they? You knew because I told you about Robert Davies.'

'Not everything, *cariad*. You only told me half of it.'

'I was twenty-three then, with most of my training finished and about to become qualified as a GP. And you were thirty. I loved you like a sister, Ellen, and I told you as much as I could about Robert. But I was too miserable to tell you everything. Now I'm twenty-seven and determined to put all that behind me. So I don't really want to rake it all up again.'

'But this man. Your colleague, as you called him the other day. Hasn't he become—well, special to you?'

He had, without her really knowing. But she didn't want him to figure in her life at all. As far as she was concerned, tangling with men always brought heartache in the end. It didn't matter what kind of relationship they entered into, after a while they managed to destroy it just because of their very nature.

'Of course he isn't special,' she said doggedly. 'What on earth gave you that idea?'

Ellen smiled, her voice soft as she said, 'It's the way you look at him. And the way he looks at you when you don't notice. I think he's in love with you, Eryl.'

'That's nonsense! He's a widower. The kind who'll never forget his wife. I'm sure she must have meant everything to him, otherwise he'd be married again by this time, wouldn't he? After all, he's well past the thirty mark.'

Ellen smiled knowingly. 'You just listen to me, Eryl. His temper is bad because he wants you to love him and thinks you don't.'

'You should be writing romantic poetry, Ellen! Not working on a farm.'

Suddenly Mrs Pugh spoke. She had been sitting there so quietly that Eryl had almost forgotten her.

'I agree with Ellen,' she said, sounding like some wise old soothsayer. 'You, *merchi cariad*, are not seeing what's under your very nose.'

At that moment Llew arrived, offering to take Eryl back to the surgery. She said goodbye to Mrs Pugh, promising to do what she could about hospital accommodation and then swore to herself that if she found any difficulty she would consult Trefor Dillon about it.

She also promised herself to forget all that nonsense the Pughs had spoken. Lewis in love with her? It was nothing but moonshine! They didn't know what they were talking about.

But somehow, as Llew drove her down the mountain and on to Dynas, their words just wouldn't go away.

That evening, because there were fewer patients than usual, Eryl finished her surgery early. At eight o'clock she told Betty Williams that she was now free to sort out the patients on Lewis Caswell's list.

Betty looked surprised. 'But he's already got through them. He left here some time ago.'

'But I thought he was in Swanton. In fact, he asked me to take over the last time I saw him.'

'Oh, that! Yes, he was there. But he returned ages ago. Must have forgotten to tell you he was back.'

Forgotten? That was hardly likely. 'So where is he?'

Betty shrugged. 'Presumably at home. Although—no, wait a minute. He did say something about dropping in on Dr Dillon before he left. You might just catch him if you hurry.'

Eryl made her way to the main house, her heart thumping uncomfortably. Although she had planned to consult Trefor about Mrs Pugh staying in Swanton Hospital, she most certainly hadn't envisaged meeting Lewis face to face. Not yet, while her feelings were still so raw. Her hand hesitated over the buzzer as she debated whether or not to see Trefor tonight. Then, deciding that she really couldn't let Mrs Pugh down by delaying things, she pressed it.

The door opened at once without her having to speak her name. She realised this had happened because someone was being shown out by Mrs Reynolds.

At that moment the worst of her scenarios came to life and she found herself colliding with Lewis.

'*You*!' he said, an angry light in his eyes.

'Excuse me,' she said politely, skirting round him as she stepped into the hall. She smiled at the housekeeper, asking if Trefor was still up.

'He's just about to go to bed,' she said. 'But seeing it's you, my dear, I can see no reason to send you away. But don't spend too long with him, will you? He's very tired.'

Lewis, who was still hovering in the hall, frowned at her as he said, 'It might be wiser if you left your visit till tomorrow.'

'Really? Perhaps we should let Trefor be the judge of that.'

Lewis stared at her for a moment before turning

towards the door. 'Just as you like,' he said sourly. Then he left without another word.

She suddenly became aware of Mrs Reynolds giving her what she could only describe as 'a look'. 'Is Dr Dillon worse?' she asked, suddenly becoming breathless.

'Oh, no, my dear. A little better, in fact. But he's just had what one might call a very difficult time. So he's really more than ready for bed.'

Eryl didn't need to ask what the woman really meant. She felt instinctively that it was Lewis who had caused this 'difficult time' and only hoped that he hadn't upset the old man too much.

'I'll be as quick as I can,' she said, hurrying to the sitting-room where she knew Trefor would be. When she went in she was appalled by what she saw. Looking absolutely exhausted, the doctor was lying back in an armchair with his eyes closed.

She called his name softly, then touched his hand. 'It's me,' she said, 'come to see how you are.'

His eyes opened with difficulty but he managed a smile at the sight of her. 'You do my old heart good, *cariad*,' he said. 'Come and sit near me like you usually do. Then you can tell me your version of the Pugh saga. So far I've only heard what happened from Dr Caswell. And I must say it didn't make good listening.'

There was no need to ask what he and Lewis had been discussing nor how the wretched man had managed to upset this wonderful old doctor. 'It shouldn't have happened,' she said softly. 'I shouldn't have jumped the gun like I did.'

He chuckled softly. 'Oh, yes, you should, my dear. If you think you're right you should stick by what you want to do. But promise me one thing, *merchi*.'

She smiled. 'When I come to see you I always seem to end up making you promises. What is it this time?'

His own smile was wicked. 'Whatever you do, Eryl, when you have a good idea like getting Mrs Pugh accommodation in hospital with her husband please ask Lewis about it first. Then, if you can manage it, allow him to believe he was the first to think of it.'

She was stunned for a moment. She said in a strangled voice, 'But why should I do that? And how could I have done it anyway when he wasn't there while I spoke to Mrs Pugh?'

Trefor sighed. 'I'm afraid you have a lot to learn about your colleague. I told you long ago how complicated he is. How shy at heart. What I didn't tell you, because it wouldn't have been right at that time, was how damaged he is.'

She stayed silent, trying to digest this picture of the man she so often found merely bad-tempered. And, strangely enough, it fitted in with those pictures she'd had of him when they'd eaten lunch together in his cottage.

'So, what happened to him?' she asked.

Trefor sighed, staying silent for a moment. Then at last he said, 'It's all to do with his wife, I'm afraid. She caused him such heartache, you see.'

'I realise he's not fully over her death. But. . .'

'It's not only that, *merchi*. There's more. But I don't really want to betray a confidence, my dear. All I ask is for you to be gentle with him, however angry he is sometimes. Maybe one day he'll tell you everything.'

She began to feel a burning sensation at the back of her eyes. We have been behaving like spoilt children instead of adult doctors, she thought, disgusted with

herself for her part in it. All she had achieved was
a show of anger from a colleague who should be a
workmate, not an enemy. But more than this she had
caused this wonderful old man a kind of suffering that
he didn't deserve.

'I'm sorry,' she said softly. 'I'll try to be more tactful
with Lewis in future. That is if he can ever bring himself
to speak to me again.'

'He was angry with you on his way out?'

'That's putting it mildly.'

Trefor began to laugh softly. 'He'll come round,' he
said. 'He can't afford to lose you.'

Eryl couldn't ask Trefor what he meant by this
because at that moment his laugh turned into a harsh
dry cough. She didn't like the sound of it at all and
asked sharply, 'Has that been with you long?'

He rose to his feet still spluttering but managed to
say it was time he went to bed.

'I asked you a question, Doctor,' she said, more
quietly this time, 'about that nasty little cough.'

He tried to shrug it off. 'Oh, that! I've had it for a
few days, perhaps. But that's all. I just need a packet
of lozenges. Or something more appropriate for my
second childhood, like jelly babies!'

'Has Lewis prescribed something for it?'

'No. For the simple reason I've never coughed in
front of him.'

'Then I'll have a word with him, shall I?'

Trefor smiled at her, walking slowly towards the
door. 'If you like, my dear. But please go gently with
him. Promise me?'

She looked at him with love in her heart. 'I promise,'
she said.

*   *   *

There was one unexpected advantage that grew out of that ill-fated visit to the Pughs' farm. After learning that the family had to drive miles down the mountain to fetch the ambulance service, Lewis insisted that the three doctors in Dynas should be issued with mobile phones. That way, when they were visiting patients they could keep in touch with the surgery, he said, to say nothing of vital services such as Mountain Rescue and the police. Trefor agreed and they were ordered immediately.

Soon after that, one afternoon in early August, Trefor asked his staff to shelve visits and anything else they had planned so that they could gather in his surgery for a meeting. This was the first time that he had left the house for any length of time since his collapse and Eryl tried to keep a wary eye on him as he settled into a chair behind his desk.

But, sitting next to Nerys, she was torn between concentrating on the old doctor and listening to what the young nurse was saying to her in an undertone. At last Nerys won, telling Eryl in a series of hoarse whispers that she and Doug were expecting their first baby.

At first Eryl felt cold with shock—seeing a vivid picture of herself as she might have been if only Robert hadn't walked out of her life. But an instant later her common sense took over, making her see how empty that old routine of 'if only' always was. Pushing aside the envy she felt, she at last admitted to herself that she felt genuinely pleased for Nerys and Doug. 'That's terrific!' she said. 'Can I be godmother?'

Trefor suddenly rapped on his desk and asked, 'Are we ready, you two? Perhaps you'd like to keep your gossip for later.'

'Sorry, Dr Dillon!' Nerys dimpled at him and then

gave everyone else a smile that she just couldn't keep to herself.

Looking puzzled, Trefor asked, 'Is there something I should know about, my dear?'

'Yes, I think perhaps there is. It's early days yet but—Doug and I are going to become parents.'

After that there was no way that Trefor could begin his meeting. Everyone began to chatter at once, congratulating Nerys loudly in both Welsh and English. The other nurse, Liz Brown, left her seat to give Nerys a hug and the two receptionists smiled at her, looking as if they'd both won the national lottery.

The only person to stay aloof was Lewis. When everything had quietened down Eryl saw him sitting motionless, a bleak look in his eyes.

Nerys smiled at him and said, 'Well, Dr Caswell! Aren't you going to wish me luck, too?'

He pulled himself together, then focused his attention on the nurse, looking as if he'd just returned from that long and difficult journey inside himself that Eryl had witnessed before. 'Of course,' he said at last. 'I hope everything goes well for you.'

But he sounded dispirited, as if he found the words hard to speak. Almost as if he *hated* children, Eryl thought suddenly. Yet this was sheer nonsense. His young patients really liked him and most of the teenagers she'd seen leaving his surgery frankly adored him. They wouldn't have responded this way if he'd shown only the surly side of his nature, would they?

At last she pushed all these disturbing thoughts aside, giving her full attention to Trefor as he asked, 'Does this mean we'll have to start looking for a replacement for you, young Nerys?'

'Only temporarily, Doctor. After maternity leave I

hope to be back. Doug's mother says she'll take over whenever I want her to. She can hardly wait to be with her first grandchild, in fact.'

The meeting then began in earnest, with Trefor congratulating Lewis on having thought of using mobile phones. 'Personally I think we should all carry them, nurses included,' he said. 'Then if we find an emergency we can't deal with in some remote region we'll be able to call for help. Oh, I know they present difficulty in some mountainous areas but we can always overcome that by driving to a place where they'll function properly.'

'You say "we", Dr Dillon,' Eryl said. 'Does this mean you now feel well enough to return to work?'

'Of course! I've spent too long doing nothing. It's high time I shared the load again.'

Eryl saw Lewis frown as he said, 'I don't think that's a good idea, Doctor. We haven't really resolved the reason for your collapse, have we? Nor got rid of that weakness you still feel.'

Trefor began to look agitated. 'Then isn't it time you got on with it?' he said, his voice unusually sharp. 'By now you should have stirred up all those specialists you know. So far they've just fobbed you off, trying this and that with me. As if they were dealing with some sort of guinea pig, for God's sake! Then coming up with the most outlandish diagnoses I've ever heard.'

Lewis sighed. 'They're doing their best, Doctor, but they still find you something of a mystery.'

'Well, they shouldn't! Medical science has advanced a great deal since I first became a GP. So why all this delay? Just tell me that!' He paused, waiting for Lewis to offer an explanation. When he didn't Trefor stood up and rapped his knuckles on the desk. 'I'll tell you why, my boy! It's because there's nothing wrong with me, except for a touch of Anno Domini! And we all know that treating people as if they were past it only makes them grow old quicker.'

He sat down, suddenly looking stricken as he had to fight for breath. Then he began to cough, making that dry, harsh sound that had worried Eryl the night she had returned from the Pughs'.

She rose swiftly and went to the back of his chair, holding his shoulders steady.

Lewis said loudly, 'What's all this, Dr Dillon? Something you've been hiding from me?'

Trefor twisted his shoulders irritably, moving them from Eryl's grasp. Unable to speak, he pointed to her seat, indicating that she should go back to it which she did but only with reluctance.

Dr Dillon then tried to glare at Lewis but failed, finally sneezing several times and leaning back in his seat with an expression of despair etched on his face.

When he had eventually grown quiet he gave Lewis the saddest look that Eryl thought she had ever seen. It also seemed to be tinged with guilt. 'So, you've at last found me out!' he said, his voice little more than a grating whisper. 'I didn't tell you about this before because I expected it to vanish.'

Eryl wondered how often doctors had heard their patients speak this way, only to curse the courage that had led them to put up with conditions that could be cured—or at least contained—with early treatment.

She got up and went to Trefor again, this time helping him to his feet. 'I'll take you back to the house,' she said softly. 'Then Mrs Reynolds can make you a cup of nice strong tea.'

Giving her a wicked look, he said, 'How very Welsh

of you, my dear. What would we Celts do without tea that comes out of the pot looking like treacle?'

Later that day Trefor was taken into hospital again. This time he bypassed Pandy, going straight to Swanton for further and even more rigorous tests for his heart and arteries. But, after a week, Dr Smith again ruled out coronary disease.

When Eryl was about to leave the hospital after visiting Trefor one afternoon the young registrar took her into a side room. 'I find this case more than baffling,' he confessed, then told her that further tests done by his colleague on the doctor's urine showed sugar levels that were now normal. 'But I don't propose to stop here. I've already consulted with everyone else you could name so we're all set to give him even more tests until we get to the bottom of this mystery.'

Consequently Trefor was exposed to every examination doctors in various departments saw fit to carry out. In the end his liver, his kidneys and his blood count showed nothing unusual or sinister. Tests for allergies ruled out many common causes of other symptoms, such as the sneezing fits he had developed along with the cough that had worried everybody at the meeting in Dynas.

After all this every doctor and scientist involved reluctantly came to the conclusion that there seemed to be nothing wrong with him. Even the rasping cough subsided dramatically, just as Trefor had predicted. Yet he continued to feel as tired as before.

'Is there *nothing* more we can do?' Eryl asked, feeling thoroughly exasperated.

Dr Smith gave a hopeless shrug. 'We've done everything. Blood tests. X-rays. The lot.'

'So—how are his lungs? You did X-ray those, I presume.'

'That's really Dr Hopkins's department. I X-rayed his chest for his heart but I left the X-ray of his lungs to Hopkins. If there was anything there he would have told me.'

Eryl wasn't satisfied with this. It sounded too vague. She considered Swanton to be a better than average place but just the same lines sometimes got crossed, didn't they? Communication could go astray despite the best intentions.

She said, 'It's that dry cough that concerns me more than anything else. I know it's a little better but it's still there. Is it possible that. . .?' She paused, not wanting to tread on this man's toes by suggesting that someone might have been negligent.

'Go on,' he said pleasantly. 'Please feel free to speak your mind. Trefor Dillon would be the first to tell you that, I'm sure.'

'Well, then—the lung X-ray. Is it possible to have missed something there?'

Smith looked at her in silence for a few moments. Then he said, 'I'll have a word with Hopkins. You never know. Even a lung man as good as he is is only human. It isn't as if an X-ray can shout at you, is it?'

She left it there, hoping that someone, somewhere, might find an answer. And hoped that if they did, they would be in time to also find a remedy.

CHAPTER NINE

LEWIS and Eryl both visited the hospital regularly, although they never managed to arrive together. Eryl suspected that this was intentional on his part. That even though they were now working together fairly amicably Lewis had no wish to be left in her company for too long. And certainly not socially.

This saddened her. But after a while she saw it as a relief. At least she wasn't on tenterhooks all the time, trying not to upset his volatile nature. Yet at other times she considered it to be a loss because she missed discussing general aspects of medicine with him. Missed talking over problems, too, like the very real one that she was now facing with Lewis's ex-patient, David Morland.

After an initially good start with the recluse, where she had almost persuaded him to undergo a series of stomach scans, he had suddenly refused to see her when she called at the caravan. Losing contact with a patient whom she considered desperately needed help, she wanted to consult Lewis professionally.

But, not only that, she found that she also missed his company. She wanted to laugh with him as she had done not so long ago. Even wanted to share the cats with him because he seemed to love them as much as she did.

And then one afternoon their visits to Swanton coincided. He had called in to see Gareth Pugh, who was still there even though his damaged ankle had now

127

healed well. This delay in signing him out was because
the man had at last been persuaded to have tests for his
enlarged prostate. A biopsy showed no sign of carci-
noma but despite this the swollen gland was removed
to save further trouble.

Eryl, also visiting Gareth after calling in on Trefor,
became aware of someone talking to the staff nurse
sitting at a desk near the entrance to the ward.

She looked up quickly to see Lewis there and suddenly found herself unable to move. He'd been absent
for some days, disappearing in that mysterious way
that puzzled her despite her resolve to ignore it.

Now, as if his eyes were drawn to her by some
invisible magnet, he turned to stare at her. With irritation, she thought, as if he questioned her right to be
here with his patient. But as their gazes became locked
she saw other emotions flitting over those eyes, his
face holding something that looked remarkably like
pleasure. That rapidly disappeared, to be replaced by
amazement.

Walking slowly towards her, he said, 'What on earth
are you doing here?'

'The same as you, it seems. Visiting Gareth Pugh.'

'But——he's not your patient!'

'I've come to see Gareth as a friend,' she said hastily,
'and to give Mrs Pugh a lift back home.'

'But she's staying here, isn't she? I seem to remember you winning that particular battle.'

Taken by themselves, his words could have sounded
like an insult. But, noticing a faint twinkle of amusement in his eyes, she smiled at him and thanked
whatever god of medicine was guarding his volatile
tongue when he smiled back.

'She *was* staying here. But not any longer. When

Gareth began to recover from his surgery she decided she'd be more use at home. So I've been bringing her in to see him whenever I could.'

'So, where is she now?'

Gareth said something in Welsh and Eryl laughed.

'What was that?' Lewis's voice was sharp, filled with the suspicion that was always with him when people talked in the language he refused to learn. Because it was too hard, he'd once told her.

Eryl laughed again, then told Gareth that he was being wicked. In English she said to Lewis, 'His wife is in the cloakroom. Prettying herself up, as he puts it. He told me how vain she's become lately. How he even suspects her of having a lover, would you believe?'

Lewis stared at her. Then he said quite seriously, 'Is that possible? Does that sort of thing really go on with mountain folk?'

She couldn't believe that he really meant it. But he suddenly looked so dejected that she stretched out her hand, touching his without thinking. Then she wished she hadn't for, as his fingers turned to thread themselves through hers, she felt a tingle run up her arm as if his body was charged with electricity.

Hastily she took her hand away and said, 'Of course it doesn't happen here! What makes you think an upright, chapel-going family like the Pughs would live like that?'

'They're human, aren't they? In my experience, most people have the power to betray others.'

He was leaning towards her, speaking softly so that Gareth couldn't follow what he was saying. And the desperation that she heard in his voice hurt her. He sounded as if he was speaking personally. As if he, himself, was no stranger to betrayal.

And then the tense moment passed as Mrs Pugh returned from the cloakroom. Seeing both doctors there, she asked how Dr Dillon was progressing.

Eryl looked enquiringly at Lewis, who shook his head slightly and came out with the usual cliché doctors made when they weren't certain of something. 'He's as well as can be expected,' he said.

Mrs Pugh looked relieved but Eryl stiffened. This sort of term usually meant the opposite and for her it wasn't good enough. 'Why don't you say what you really mean?' she said brusquely, choosing a moment when Mrs Pugh couldn't possibly hear because she had closed the curtains around the bed and was now helping her husband into clean pyjamas.

'I can't say anything better than that because I don't know what else to tell her,' Lewis said. 'I've just discovered that after Hopkins X-rayed Trefor's lungs he took only a hurried look at the result, intending to go back to it later. But, in the meantime, the girls in charge of the filing department mislaid it.'

'*What*?'

'Yes, you may well exclaim.'

'But how did that happen, for God's sake?'

'It just happened, that's all!' He began to sound so angry that Eryl thought he would explode and she really couldn't blame him. Then he said more calmly, 'But I've sorted all that out at last. Trefor's down in X-ray now for a second one. The results should be up here any minute. Want to wait and see them for yourself?'

'Yes, but I can't because of taking Mrs Pugh home.'

'Get her a cup of tea or something. Suggest she stays with her husband for a little longer.'

'You're sure you want me here?'

He studied her face for a moment and once again

she saw that strange mix of emotions flitting across his eyes. And she wondered, suddenly, why she had ever wished to push him out of her life.

At last he said quietly, 'Of course I want you here. Probably more than you'll ever realise.'

She didn't know how to look at him and wished that he could always be like this—receptive and caring, with none of his abrasive nature showing. She left him to go back to Mrs Pugh and arrange for a cup of tea to be brought to her, promising to pick her up as soon as she could.

On her way to see Trefor she found Lewis by a reception desk with Dr Smith and Dr Hopkins, the 'lung man' who was supposed to be so good. They had fixed Trevor's latest X-ray to a lighted stand and were silently examining the results.

As Eryl stood beside them Lewis introduced her briefly to Dr Hopkins, who nodded at her and fixed another X-ray alongside the latest one.

'Thank God the original turned up in time to save my bacon,' he said, explaining to Eryl how it had eventually been found filed in the wrong place. Then he asked if she could see anything unusual in the X-ray.

She was about admit that everything looked perfectly normal to her when she suddenly saw a minute shadow in the latest picture that wasn't anywhere in the first. Pointing to it, she said, 'Surely this is a new development, isn't it?'

Hopkins was now giving her a broad smile. 'You've got quick eyes, haven't you? When I saw it just now I thought I'd been mistaken.'

'What is it?' she asked. 'TB? Or something more—sinister?'

'Frankly, I don't know exactly what it is. It can't be

TB because that would have been spotted in the blood tests. As for the big C I think it's highly unlikely. This shadow presents more like some kind of fungus, I should have thought.'

'Fungus?' Lewis said. 'Well, I'll be damned!'

'You've met this sort of thing before?' Hopkins asked.

'Yes. In Africa. Quite frequently. But never in this country.' Lewis turned to Eryl. 'Did you ever come across this in the Midlands, Doctor?'

'Not really. Though a colleague treated an immigrant suffering from a type of lupus which had spread to his lungs. He'd contracted the disease in his home country but it wasn't discovered until he arrived in Birmingham.'

'I somehow feel that lupus isn't the culprit. We'd have picked that up in the blood tests.' Hopkins thought deeply for a moment, then he said, 'This could be something quite rare, though not unheard-of in rural areas. If I was a gambling man I'd lay a bet on it being caused by *Aspergillus fumigatus*. Devilish little creatures that colonise to form a fungus ball. Oh, they're clever they are. Go undetected for a long time. But of course I'd want to do further tests before I made up my mind.'

'Such as?' Lewis asked.

Hopkins shrugged. 'If the fungus had actually colonised, forming a ball, then a biopsy is indicated. But, looking at the X-ray, I don't think it's gone that far. A specific blood test should give us the answer.'

Eryl had come across this condition in textbooks but had never met it in a patient. And never in anyone as wonderful as Trefor, she thought, suddenly feeling the prickle of tears behind her eyes.

'Is there a cure?' she asked shakily, then had to turn away and swallow hard.

'Oh, yes, there certainly is,' Hopkins said. 'A course of specialised antibiotics will clear up the condition. It'll take time, of course, but it will succeed in the end, I promise you.'

She felt a hand on her arm and turned to see Lewis looking deep into her eyes, which were still stinging. 'Hold on in there!' he said softly. 'You mustn't let Trefor see you looking like this.'

Of course she mustn't! Where on earth was that professional face that she always donned when talking to patients? She smiled faintly at Lewis and said, 'Trefor won't see me in this state, I promise.'

'That's my girl! Save your weeping for when you get home. Then we'll have some very strong coffee. And talk together. It's been too long since we did that, hasn't it?'

After leaving the hospital Eryl and Lewis arrived in Dynas separately, he just in time for evening surgery and Eryl a little late, having first taken Mrs Pugh home.

But, despite her rush, she sat quietly in her room for a while, trying to steady herself before calling in her first patient.

Ever since Lewis had spoken to her in Swanton she had been in a dream-like state that made her feel as if she were not really part of this world. In a way it was exciting yet it was also unnerving for no matter how hard she tried to hide away from it the feeling just wouldn't leave her. It fired her imagination and conjured up impossible scenarios in her mind that left her breathless one moment and irritated with herself the next.

At last, unable to bear her thoughts any longer, she called for the first person on her list. But the image of Lewis, with that gentle compassion etched on his face as he looked into her eyes, was still with her.

Tonight there seemed to be more patients than usual, many of them coming in for the most trivial reasons. Forcing herself to give each person the attention they deserved, she dealt with nothing more serious than sore throats, colds that wouldn't go away and slight headaches that certainly didn't merit anything stronger than aspirin. And as she met one patient after another she gradually saw the strong coffee and talk that Lewis had promised disappearing.

Then something occurred that Eryl had hoped wouldn't happen in Dynas, even though Trefor Dillon had warned her about it when she first arrived. A young mother walked in with a small boy who was literally smothered in chickenpox blisters.

It was a single appointment for the mother, Eryl noted, but because the child was also here the reception-ist had added his card. Hastily scanning both, Eryl saw that the young woman had been treated for a sore throat by Trefor some time before his collapse and her small son had been visited by Lewis one night when he was on call.

Frowning at the mother, Eryl said severely, 'Mrs Rees, I'm surprised to see little Jamie with you. You do realise that he's still highly infectious, don't you? It's not really safe to take him out until those blisters stop weeping and turn into scabs.'

'I couldn't help it, Doctor! There's no one to look after him, see. And my throat's so sore again I just had to come.' She was whining and looking sorry for herself. Then she gave Eryl an insolent grin and said, 'Anyway, it's Miss, not Mrs.'

'Have you got a partner?' Eryl asked, hoping that the girl at least had someone to stand by her.

'Not now. He left.'

Eryl drew in a sharp breath, feeling a swift compassion for this young mother. This could so nearly have been her own story, couldn't it?

'So, what about your mother? Would she be able to look after the child while you're out?'

'Huh! Not a hope! She's gone, too. Walked out with *my* guy, if you please! Says he's her toy boy and all that garbage.' She sniffed, then glared at Eryl as if everything was her fault. 'Should have known better at her age!'

Eryl found all this hard to understand. If she'd been in the Midlands she wouldn't have been surprised. But here? In Dynas, where everything seemed so ordinary? So peaceful?

Then she thought back to her own young days and the temptations that had always been around, just as they were in other places. And she suddenly saw an image of Robert, telling her to trust him and that everything would be all right once they were together. And then leaving her, not only with a heart that seemed to die but with all the problems that he had brought her and had refused to sort out.

'I'm sorry,' she said, knowing how inadequate this must sound but meaning it sincerely. 'Have you talked to the Social Welfare people?'

'Don't want charity, thanks very much!'

'But how do you manage to live? Earn money?'

'That's easy, Doctor. There's one good thing Mam taught me. Like most Welsh folk I can knit. And old

Lloyd sells my stuff for me in his shop. He's even promised to get me a knitting machine an' show me how to use it.'

Surprised, Eryl said, 'You know him well, then?'

The girl laughed, a happy tinkling sound that seemed so incongruous after her recital of misery. 'Should do!' she said. 'He's Mam's grandad.'

Eryl stared at the girl, amazed. Then she vaguely remembered her as a very young and feisty teenager, hanging around the village with a number of likely lads.

'Did you sit near anyone else in the waiting-room?' she asked.

'No. Mrs Jones wanted us to go to what she called the ice room, whatever that is.'

Eryl hid a smile and said, 'Isolation room.'

'Right. But it was being used, see. So she made us wait outside till our turn. Why all the bloomin' fuss, I just don't know!'

Suddenly irritated by the girl's cavalier attitude, Eryl said sharply, 'I'll tell you why! Chickenpox isn't particularly dangerous for your son but if older people come into contact with the disease they're quite likely to develop shingles. And that could turn out to be very nasty indeed.'

She saw the bravado leave the girl's face, instantly replaced by a look of fear, and thought that her message had at last got through. But a moment later she realised how wrong she was. Miss Rees seemed to be concerned only for herself.

'Does that mean I could get these shingle things, too? What are they, anyway?' she asked.

'Something that can be even more painful than chickenpox. So if you develop any blisters like Jamie's, particularly around your waist, just stay indoors and ask for a home visit.'

'Right, Doctor. I will.'

Eryl washed her hands at the sink, took a wooden spatula and examined the girl's throat. It looked raw but didn't present any white patches that could indicate the need for antibiotics so she suggested a well-known antiseptic gargle, which could be bought over the counter of any chemist.

While she was washing her hands again she said, 'How is young Jamie sleeping?'

'Very bad, Doctor. Neither of us gets a decent night.' The girl stood up, already moving towards the door.

Eryl called her back. 'Just wait while I write a pre-scription, will you? I'm giving you a mild sedative for Jamie to help him to sleep but I'm afraid I can't pre-scribe the lotion you should be dabbing on his blisters. So you must promise me to get some calamine from the chemist, along with the gargle I mentioned. And *please* ask a neighbour to look after Jamie while you're out, will you?'

'OK, Doc! I promise.' The girl waited impatiently while Eryl wrote up the script and stuffed it into her pocket. 'Thanks a lot,' she said cheerfully, leading her son to the door. Just before she left she turned back to give a cheeky smile and said, 'See you!' As if she hadn't a care in the world, Eryl thought.

Sighing, she told herself that it was high time she set up the hygiene clinic Trefor had promised. But until that happened it was no good worrying about patients who didn't seem to have the first idea about passing on infection. So she decided to push it out of her mind and relax for the rest of the evening.

Stretching wearily and running her hands through

her hair, she massaged her scalp which had grown uncomfortably tight. Then she looked at her watch and frowned. It was all of nine o'clock and she doubted if she would share coffee and talk with Lewis tonight. She even doubted that he was still in the building.

After handing in her notes at Reception, she made her way slowly to the courtyard. Her mind was crammed with the many things that had happened during the day and as they swirled senselessly around her brain she recognised the symptoms of exhaustion. Who was it who had said, 'Physician, heal thyself'? Some biblical prophet? Or Shakespeare, perhaps? Whoever it was the quotation fitted her present state perfectly. For no one else could put a stop to these stupid obsessional thoughts that refused to be still.

Because she had come back so late from the hospital she had opened the door of her flat, snatched what she needed for tonight's surgery from the hall table and hurried to the other building without turning on the outside light. Now clutching her medical case under one arm, she delved into a shoulder bag and fumbled for her key.

'Peace is what I need,' she said aloud, then chuckled quietly, hoping that no one had overheard her.

A shadow suddenly detached itself from her front door and her hand flew automatically to her mouth as a shiver of fear ran down her back.

A moment later she heard a voice say, 'I agree. You certainly need peace. But what you need more at the moment is food.'

'Lewis! Oh, my God, you startled me! I didn't expect you to. . .'

He moved towards her, snaking one arm around her shoulders as if he thought that she was about to fall.

'You thought I'd leave before that fine conversation I promised you over coffee?' There was a smile in his voice which made her mouth turn up at the corners in response. 'How could you be so faint-hearted, woman?'

'That offer was made ages ago, Lewis. Before anyone could guess at the size of my surgery tonight.'

'Careful!' Lewis said as she began to totter. He took the key gently from her and fitted it into the lock. Opening the door, he said, 'Wait here while I switch on the outside light. By the way, d'you mind if I put these in your oven to warm up?'

She couldn't see what he was holding in his other hand but thought that it smelt delicious. 'Fish and chips?' she asked and her fatigue began to drift away.

'Yes. I thought they would do us both a power of good, as Trefor would say.'

She laughed. 'So he's used that phrase on you, too!'

'Of course.' He moved past her and as he began to climb the stairs he said, 'I'll put these to keep warm while you make coffee. I'll also cut us some bread and butter in true traditional style.' Halfway up, he stopped. Then, sounding hesitant, he added, 'You don't mind me making myself at home like this, do you?'

'No, of course not,' she said, surprised to find that she meant it.

The light came on, flooding the courtyard and also illuminating Ladykins as she appeared from behind a bush. Seeing Eryl, the cat greeted her with a series of ecstatic chirrups and hurried up the stairs, followed by her multicoloured family who all seemed to be growing larger every day.

As soon as Eryl went into the kitchen Lewis said, 'Sit down and leave everything to me. You look bushed.' The smile that he gave her was so warm that she hadn't the heart to object, even though he was being bossy. 'Tell me—does Ladykins always wait for you like that? Why doesn't she use her splendid new cat flap?'

'It's really uncanny. If I haven't fed her for ages she knows there's nothing up here for her and waits downstairs to remind me. She's so intelligent, that animal! Affectionate, too.'

'Cupboard love!' he retorted. 'D'you want me to feed her straight away? Or shall I get on with our supper first?'

'They'll all make a fuss if they have to wait. I'll open a tin before I make coffee.'

She turned away from him, using the cats as an excuse for not facing those dark eyes that were filled with a myriad expressions again. Ranging from sheer kindness to a gentle amusement, as if he found her funny, they then reflected all those unspoken questions that she had seen so often before.

And as she dished out food into separate bowls and set them on the floor she wondered how unwise it was to be here alone with him. She felt so vulnerable tonight. Not strong enough to fend off the emotion she sensed in him.

When the cats were eating she turned her attention to making coffee and was suddenly swept back to that other time when she had cried and he had shown the kind of sympathy that could so easily have turned into love.

And she saw again his sudden and inexplicable rejection of her and felt the quiet brutality of it, which suddenly turned her life into the kind of hell she thought she had left behind when she went to England.

After he had put the fish and chips onto two plates and placed them in a lighted oven, he laid trays with cutlery and began to slice a loaf. Suddenly she found she couldn't move her gaze away from his hands. They were strong and yet so delicate at the same time—each movement precise, the long fingers supple.

He caught her looking at them and raised one eyebrow in surprise so she said hastily, 'Did you ever think of becoming a surgeon?'

'Why do you ask?'

'Your hands. That's all.'

He laughed. 'Just look at the thickness of this bread and tell me I'd be any better at the operating table!'

She smiled, feeling a sense of release because the atmosphere had lightened. 'Maybe it wasn't such a good idea!' she said. 'Shall I butter these?'

'Certainly not. I intend to wait on you tonight. So go into the sitting-room and plonk yourself in a chair.' As she hesitated he raised the knife and wagged it at her. 'Do as you're told, woman. Or else!'

They ate in the sitting-room, balancing trays on their knees. When they had finished Eryl took their empty plates into the kitchen, coming back to serve coffee. She placed his cup on a small table near his chair and took hers to another, sitting opposite him. Then they relaxed, talking for what seemed like hours.

Lewis touched on the subject of Trefor, sounding hopeful about his chances of a full recovery. Afterwards he spoke about their new phone system and eventually mentioned David Morland, the patient Eryl had taken over from him, and asked how she was getting on with him.

'I'm glad you mentioned him,' she said. 'I've been

wanting to talk to you about him for some time.'

'Oh? Experiencing difficulties there?'

She sighed. 'You could say that. He just won't accept the fact that he needs further investigation for those stomach pains. I don't think I've ever met such an obstinate man!'

'But I thought you were getting on so well with him.'

'I was. Then suddenly, out of the blue, he as good as told me to get lost.'

'What? After that battle you won? Frightening the life out of him with the threat of court cases and so on?'

'Yes. I can't understand it.'

Lewis looked at her curiously for a moment. Then he said, 'Has it ever occurred to you that. . .?'

'That what?'

He twitched his shoulders impatiently. 'Forget it! It was an insane idea, anyway.'

'Go on, Lewis. Tell me.'

After hesitating for a moment he looked at her, his brown eyes steady and solemn. Then he said quietly, 'Do you think—well, that he might have fallen in love with you?'

Her eyes widened. '*Lewis*! That's a crazy thing to say! He wouldn't risk flouting ethics like that, even if he felt that way. Besides, in spite of all your hints about him being a womaniser, I just don't believe he's that sort of man.'

'He's clever, though. Intelligent enough to sever the doctor-patient relationship before—well, before declaring himself.'

Eryl laughed with genuine amusement. 'You make him sound like some Edwardian dandy! Declaring himself, indeed!'

But Lewis looked far from amused. She saw his eyes

snap with something that seemed very like anger. Then
they changed, becoming even darker as they filled with
a kind of sadness that she just couldn't explain. Was
this what Trefor had meant when he'd spoken about
Lewis being damaged? Had his wife given him cause
for the jealousy that she suddenly glimpsed in him?

At last he said, 'Would you mind if that happened?
Do you feel—attracted to him?'

'No! I most certainly do not,' she said emphatically
and wished with all her heart that he would drop the
subject.

Suddenly feeling as if she was being smothered she
stood up, ready to take their empty coffee cups to the
kitchen. Wanting to be alone. Wanting him to go. But
before she could reach for his cup he also stood, catching hold of her arm and turning her towards him.

'What kind of man does attract you, then?' he asked
softly, staring at her with a strange light burning in
his eyes.

She froze, unable to look away from him and afraid
of the touch of his hands that were now gripping both
her arms. Afraid of the sensation that was moving deep
within her. Scared of herself even more than she feared
him at this moment.

'I've already told you I was once engaged,' she said.
'Isn't that enough?'

'No. You said that was in the past. But what about
your future?'

'It's none of your damned business!' Forcing her
arms away from his hands, she glared at him. 'So get
out, will you? Just leave me alone!'

He stayed silent for a long time then. Just looking
at her as if he was trying to see right into her soul.
She waited for this mood to change—expecting him

to grow angry, to walk out and stomp down the stairs like he had done before. But he didn't.

Instead he said quietly, 'But I can't leave you alone, Eryl.'

'Why not? Do you expect me to do something foolish? Like cry all night because the man I once thought so perfect disappeared without trace?' She took in a shuddering breath. 'For God's sake, just spare me your sympathy! I'm over all that now.'

'But you're not, are you? Whoever he was he still haunts you and will go on ruining your life if you let him, even though he's no longer here.'

She felt her anger draining away. Ready to deny everything Lewis said, she knew in her heart that he was right.

She felt behind her for a chair and sank onto the edge of it, unable to stand upright any longer. 'I can't understand why you're doing this,' she said at last, her voice taut. 'You're forcing me to dig up everything I buried long ago. And what for? So that you can crow over me? Because it pleases you to see a doctor fail just because she's a woman?'

She saw him flinch and knew that she should stop. But she couldn't stem the flow of words that went on pouring out of her. 'I'm right, aren't I?' she said savagely. 'It's all to do with that prejudice of yours about women doctors. Yet, in spite of that, you married one!'

She saw his whole body grow stiff and cursed herself for speaking like this. 'I'm sorry!' she murmured. 'Please forget I said that. It was unthinking of me.'

'Maybe it was. But, then perhaps, like you, it's time I also forgot the past.'

He turned towards her again and the pain that she saw in him was more than she could bear. Without thinking, she stretched out her hand and touched his arm. And then those supple fingers that she had admired as she'd watched him cutting bread threaded themselves through hers. She didn't know how she was to resist the warmth in them and as he pulled her gently to her feet again she stared up into his face with a kind of agony sweeping through her.

This isn't fair, she thought. She was too tired to fight and felt too vulnerable to gather up her courage.

And then his arms were around her, those fingers moving over her back with a softness that she had only imagined in her dreams. Could a man really be this caring? Could this delicate gentleness live beneath such a rugged exterior?

As she went on looking into his face she saw his eyes grow darker. Yet there were no shadows in them. Nothing at all concealing his thoughts. She saw only a raw need in him—a surge of passion that could not be stilled.

'Lewis—I. . .' Her voice was so faint that she could scarcely hear it herself.

'Don't speak, Eryl,' he said. 'Don't spoil this moment with words.'

She wanted to tell him to stop but couldn't find the words. And then his lips brushed hers with a touch more gentle than she could ever have imagined and she was lost.

At last he lifted his mouth from hers and sighed, looking down at her with that strange sadness in his face that pulled at her.

'I need you, Eryl,' he said. 'You'll never know how much.'

CHAPTER TEN

WHEN Lewis uttered those words to Eryl his voice was ragged—as if he found it difficult to speak yet could not contain his need of her. She sensed a vast yearning in him which pulled at her and she wanted to assuage the hurt that she saw in him, no longer caring that the barriers she had built so carefully around herself were threatening to vanish. If she could take away his agony, even for just a short time, that was all she asked.

He hadn't spoken of love and she knew that the memory of his dead wife would always be with him but she no longer cared. If meeting his physical needs was all he asked she would learn to be content.

At last she smiled at him—gently and with hesitation. Then she brushed her lips against his cheek and said, 'I need you too, Lewis.'

As he went on staring at her silently, she put her hand in his. Leading him to her bedroom, she shut the door behind them and switched on a small lamp that sent an amber glow over the walls.

For a long time he stood quite still, looking at her without speaking. Then he murmured, 'Are you sure?'

'I want you to be happy,' she said softly. 'I can't bear to see all that pain in you.'

'But you? What if. . .?'

He didn't finish the words so she spoke them for him. 'You mean what if I fall in love with you? Don't worry, Lewis. I happen to believe that there's only ever one great love in a person's life. I've experienced that love once and so have you. I'm not looking for more.'

She saw a strange sadness creeping over his face and thought that it was because of the grief he still felt. It never occurred to her that he might be hurt by what she'd just said because she took it for granted that he was not asking for commitment.

After staring at her in silence for a moment longer he began to undress her. His hands were gentle, barely touching her flesh. Yet a warm sensation tingled over her skin as if he had actually embraced her. And all the time his fingers moved his eyes never left her face.

At last she stood there quite naked, suddenly wanting to wrap her arms around her vulnerable body to protect it. But she found that she couldn't move. She was mesmerised, held by the subtle spell he was weaving as his gaze now swept from her breasts to the smallness of her waist and down and down until his dark eyes had encompassed every part of her.

'Come here,' he said, taking her hand and moving her slowly towards him. 'Undress me. Please undress me,' he said, his voice sounding as if it came from far away.

He waited in absolute stillness as she began to take off his clothes, his eyes never leaving her face. Only when her fingers began to tremble did his hands move to help her.

When they were both completely unclothed he touched her shoulders, drawing her gently towards him until their bodies were touching and their warmth mingled as they clung together. Then he led her to the bed, pulling the covers back.

'Lie with me, Eryl,' he said huskily. 'Let us bring comfort to each other.'

As she stretched herself at his side he reached for

the sheet, ready to cover them both. But she put her hand on his, detaining it as she whispered, 'No. Not yet. I want to go on seeing you.'

His lips curved into a hesitant smile. 'Shall we leave this bedside light on, then?'

Now she found that she couldn't speak. If she did she would spoil the magic of this moment so she just nodded silently.

And then he kissed her. Gently at first but with a growing strength that sucked the breath from her body. As the warmth of his tongue sought hers she shivered with an ecstasy she thought she had forgotten long ago.

She lay quite still as his fingers trailed paths of sensation over her naked flesh, every movement sparking a magic energy deep inside her.

Then those wonderful, supple hands grew bolder and she felt them wander to regions that had lain asleep until now because she had forced them to stay dormant. As they tweaked and teased her flesh she felt her nipples springing to life and her spirit melted when they tangled with hair that had remained hidden for so long.

As the heat of his body mingled with hers she became aware of his arousal and shuddered with a kind of delight shafting through her. His hands grew stronger and she felt the ache of longing deep inside her and thrust her body towards his with an abandon that she could no longer control.

At last he entered her and she reached a climax before he had even begun to move. He waited for a while, looking down at her with a pleasure that she had never expected to see in any man's eyes.

When she relaxed at last he murmured, 'My, my! That was something else, wasn't it?' Then, touching her lips with his once more, he drove her to the peak of longing again. And as he shuddered, reaching the height of his own ecstasy, she felt her very soul being encompassed by his and cried out in an agony of delight.

Everything grew still again and she lay in the protection of his arms, watching him until at last his eyes closed in sleep.

It was then that the foolishness of what she had done struck her like a physical blow. How could she have let any man tear down those barriers that had kept her safe until now? History was repeating itself, she thought savagely. For this was the way that she had allowed Robert to enter her very soul—only to find that he had never really wanted her. And here she was, giving herself to a man who was in desperate need of healing and allowing her spirit—as well as her body— to be entranced.

This coupling had sprung from a physical need in them both. When she had told him that she wasn't looking for love she thought she had spoken the truth. But now she realised how she had deceived herself. Instead of a physical release for both of them she had been touched by his magic. And now she was overwhelmed by love—a desperate kind of love that Lewis was certainly not seeking.

Could she ignore it? Keep this knowledge from him? She glanced at him, lying there undisturbed— even by dreams—and knew that any real love that there might be in him still belonged to the woman he had married. Even though she was dead Eryl knew that the memory of her would live in Lewis's heart for ever.

She must respect the privacy he wanted and must

never allow him even to suspect what had happened to her tonight. If she did their working relationship would be destroyed beyond repair.

During the night Lewis must have switched off the lamp for when Eryl next saw him he was a mere shadow in the dawn light filtering through her window. He was dressing quietly, obviously trying not to disturb her. Nevertheless he had woken her and she sat up feeling more alive than she had done for years. Covering her nakedness with a sheet drawn inadequately over her body, she watched him covertly, loving the strength of him, the lean shape of his torso and the lithe way he moved.

Hearing the rustle of bedclothes, he paused for a moment and said softly, 'Sorry to wake you so early but I must be off.'

'But it's not even full daylight yet!' she protested.

She saw the outline of him as he turned towards her and sensed tension in him. 'If I don't go now dear old Martha Reynolds will spot me,' he said. 'And I don't have to tell you what she'd say, do I? Nor how unpleasant she could be.'

Eryl wondered how he could talk so normally after what had happened between them and felt a sudden chill touch her skin. Then she ignored it. How else could he behave? To him the night had been merely a time of much-needed release, just as it had been to her in the beginning—before she'd been stupid enough to fall in love with him.

'You'd better hurry or the sun will be up,' she said. She'd wanted her voice to sound strong and cursed herself when she heard it waver.

'Are you all right?' he asked anxiously, bending

down to see her more closely. And she thought he looked like a man torn between making a hurried retreat and wanting to linger for a while.

At that moment she wished that he would stay, whatever people thought if they saw him leaving her flat. But she wanted the decision to be his, not hers. And he'd already made up his mind, hadn't he? Otherwise he would never be dressing the moment dawn came.

'You must go!' she said, trying to sound emphatic. 'And, yes, I'm quite OK, thanks. So hurry, will you?'

He placed a kiss on his fingers and blew it towards her. Then she heard him running down the stairs and shutting the front door behind him. No breakfast; no coffee. Nothing left but the lingering scent of his wonderful body.

During the next three days she sometimes caught a glimpse of Lewis in the distance but he never sought her out.

At first she imagined that he was blaming her for what had happened between them. Then she told herself not to be so foolish. It wasn't as if she had lured him to her flat like some harpy, was it? Oh, no, he'd been the one who had stage-managed it—by buying their supper and staying with her when she'd told him to go. And then showing her such tenderness that she hadn't found it in her heart to refuse him.

After more than a week had passed she eventually found some virtue in his strange absence. At least it gave her time to come to terms with the turmoil that churned inside her every time she thought of him. Now she tried to concentrate on her workload of patients, which seemed to have increased dramatically just lately.

One morning after surgery, when Eryl was handing her notes into Reception, Glynis asked her how Trefor was doing in Swanton Hospital. Feeling guilty because she had been so tied down with work that she hadn't found time to visit the old doctor for a while, Eryl had to admit that she didn't know how he was.

'But, strictly speaking, he's Dr Caswell's case,' she said, 'so why don't you ask him? He's sure to have visited the hospital recently.'

'Well, that's just it, you see. As far as I know he's not been near Swanton for ages. He's hardly ever here, either.'

'What on earth do you mean?' Eryl was astounded.

'He had some free time owing to him so he took it. To visit someone in Dolgelly, I believe.'

The name of the place brought back a memory of something that her tired brain couldn't quite grasp. Then she dismissed it as unimportant and said, 'You mean he's *staying* there?'

'Not as far as I know. He comes in here every morning, skips off as soon as he can and then we see neither hair nor hide of him till the next day.'

'But what about his patients?'

Glynis smiled. 'Don't tell me you haven't noticed!'

'You mean—they've been shuffled over to *me*?'

'They most certainly have, my love! Dr Caswell said it would be OK so I thought he'd asked you about it. And that you'd agreed to deal with them.'

Eryl was too furious to reply but, pinning a fairly realistic smile to her face, she left the surgery block with her head held high and stalked across the courtyard. Not until she was safely inside her flat did she give way to her anger.

Then she let it rip, swearing aloud and walking up

and down her sitting-room until she thought she would wear out the carpet. Only a pitiful cry coming from Ladykins in the kitchen stopped her. But even as she hurried to dole out cat food from a half-empty tin she was still smouldering deep inside.

Then two things happened at once. The telephone rang and she discovered that the tin she was holding was the last one. That meant that she would have to do some shopping. 'And pretty damn quick!' she said aloud as she went to the phone in her bedroom. But here again she was frustrated for just as she lifted the receiver the caller rang off.

'Right, Ladykins!' she announced. 'Shopping it is. So just tell your family to wait patiently for their next meal, will you?'

She picked up the huge shopping bag that she had bought from Lloyd's, hooked her other arm through the strap of her shoulder-bag and strode to her car in the courtyard, trying to look carefree.

She saw Nerys about to get into her car. 'That's just what I need!' she told herself and tried to avoid the nurse, keeping her head well down as she unlocked the door of her own car.

But she was too late. Nerys saw her and bounded across the courtyard, a broad smile on her face. 'Are you going there, too?' she asked. 'If so, let's travel together.'

'Into Dynas, you mean?'

'No. I'm going to visit Dr Dillon. He rang just now to say he wanted to see me. Said he was going to call you, too.'

'My phone rang as I was coming out but it stopped before I could answer.'

'Must have been him. He's awfully keen to see us both as soon as possible, he said.'

'What for?' Eryl was puzzled and only hoped that this didn't mean that Trefor was feeling worse.

Nerys smiled. 'Don't look so worried, love. He's doing fine in that place. Apparently responding well to the new treatment. Should be coming home soon, he said. Then he told me he wanted to discuss some idea he thought might interest the two of us.'

At last Eryl locked her own car again and joined Nerys in hers, slinging the shopping bag into the back. When they eventually drew into the car park at Swanton Hospital she was still wondering what all this was about.

'Oh, damn!' she said as they walked into Reception. 'I meant to buy Ladykins some food on the way here. I've run out.'

'We'll get some on the way back, shall we? Might even fit in a coffee and cake session if we're lucky. There's a super café in the centre of town.'

They waited for a lift to arrive on the ground floor and when it didn't appear they grew impatient and swept up the stairs on foot. It took a while to find Trefor because he had been moved into a single side-ward.

'Does this mean he's worse?' Eryl asked a staff nurse on duty.

'Oh, no. Quite the contrary, Dr Thomas. We're very pleased with him. He just wanted a bit of peace to do some reading, he said. So we moved him.'

Relieved, she went with Nerys into a small room to find Trefor sitting in an armchair with a book on his knees. She thought that he was looking better than she had ever seen him and, taking both of his hands in hers, she squeezed them affectionately.

And, then, quite suddenly, she found herself unable to speak, because of that stupid lump rising in her throat, like it had the time she was here with Lewis. And she could hardly control the tears that she felt prickling at the back of her eyes.

Oh, please, not now! Don't let him see me like this!

She thought of the promise that she'd made to Lewis when he'd urged her to hide her feelings. And remembered the tenderness that she had seen in him then.

At last she became aware of Trefor looking at her anxiously. 'What's wrong, *merchi*?' he asked. 'You seem tired. Has that naughty Lewis been working you to death?'

She pulled herself together, managing a smile of sorts, and clung to what Trefor had asked, using it as an excuse to hide her volatile feelings. 'Yes, he certainly is working me hard. I seem to have acquired most of his patients and I don't really know why, except that he always seems to be somewhere else.'

Trefor frowned at her, looking puzzled. 'But I thought he'd told you why. I was sure he'd consulted you before he decided to take the free time owing to him.'

Then Nerys turned to Eryl with a look of amazement. 'I knew about all this so why didn't you? I saw Dr Caswell looking for you and then, when he couldn't find you, I heard him ask Betty Williams to tell you about the change.'

'Well, she didn't,' Eryl said sharply.

'Betty also arranged a new night duty roster, taking your name off and fixing it so that Lewis was the only doctor to share duties with the surgery in Pandy. He told her to do that. Said it was only fair because he wasn't in much during the day.'

Now Eryl realised why her phone hadn't rung, giving her several nights of undisturbed sleep. 'So, what happened? Why didn't Betty tell me all this?'

'I can only think it was because she went off sick soon after Lewis made these new arrangements.'

'Never mind, *merchi*!' Trefor said, smiling and flirting with her as only he could. 'Looking tired or not, it's good to see you. As I've told you so often you do me a real POG.'

She laughed. 'You'll soon be calling me a witch!'

He nodded, then winked at her deliciously, and she silently thanked that elusive god of medicine for caring enough to cure him.

'I'd like to come home soon,' he said wistfully. 'More than anything else I miss my favourite mountain. I even dream of old Cader Idris, you know. But the powers that be say I must stay here for at least another week. That's why I asked you both to come today to discuss that idea you had a long time ago, Eryl, which sadly hasn't yet borne fruit. You know—the hygiene clinic we talked about.'

'At last!' Eryl smiled at him with mischief in her eyes. 'I thought you'd forgotten all about that.'

'As if I would!' Trefor grinned impishly at her. Then he became serious as he said, 'Maybe this isn't the best time to start it, though. Not with all the extra work Lewis has let you in for.'

'Don't you believe it! I'm raring to go.'

'Well, if you say so, my dear. Let's talk over a few ideas, shall we?'

They spoke for some time, mapping out a plan whereby she and Nerys would share informal talks that hopefully would make their patients more careful of others when it came to infectious diseases.

'I think the treatment room would be the best place for all this,' Trefor said. 'But, of course, you'd have to square it with Liz Brown. Make sure she's not using the place for injections and so on. Think you could make it work, Eryl?'

'Oh, yes. We could also run antenatal sessions, couldn't we? So far we only examine pregnant women the required number of times. We really should meet them more regularly.' In danger of being carried away with enthusiasm, Eryl then added, 'I hope you don't think I'm being too pushy.'

Trefor gave her that benign smile that always managed to melt her heart. 'Of course not, my dear. I'd also like to add a suggestion of my own. For instance, what about people like that poor little Rees girl, struggling with a small son and no husband? If only we'd had the manpower and the imagination to advise on birth control she wouldn't be where she is now, would she?'

The arrival of a nurse wearing a frown on her face put an end to the discussion. 'It's really time you left my patient in peace,' she said severely.

Eryl grinned at Trefor sheepishly. 'We should have known better, shouldn't we?' she said as they both stood up to leave.

But as Nerys went towards the door he called Eryl back. 'Don't go yet, *merchi bach*. There's something I want to say to you in private. About Lewis.'

'Oh?' Letting Nerys go on without her, Eryl walked slowly back to Trefor.

'Don't look so agitated, my dear. It's just that—well, I have a feeling that he's growing very fond of you.'

'That's not really true,' she said slowly.

He sighed. 'Just the same, I'd like you to know that if he—well, shall we say if he fell in love with you nothing would make me happier.'

Eryl smiled, trying to make light of it. 'You're an old rogue. D'you know that? An old matchmaking rogue.'

He looked at her with that same wisdom she had seen in his eyes when she'd first met him in Birmingham. Then he said, 'Just mark my words, will you? And—*please* treat him gently.'

'I promise. But I think you're completely mad,' she murmured as she kissed him goodbye. Trying to still the swift beating of her heart, she went to find Nerys in the car park.

'Time for coffee and a slice of luscious cake?' the young nurse asked.

'Why not? I've no visits this afternoon. But first I really must buy some food for Ladykins before she starves to death.'

When Nerys drove into a public car park in the centre of Swanton Eryl had almost managed to control her unruly thoughts. After she had bought a dozen tins of cat food she followed her friend to a café where they could see a crowd of people inside, sitting at small tables.

'What a crush! Must be their wonderful cakes,' Nerys said, staring enviously through the window. 'Shall we find somewhere else?'

'No. Look, there's an empty table in that far corner.'

They both went in and sat down. After stuffing the shopping bag beneath the table, they gave their order. Now positive that she had thrust all Trefor's nonsense behind her Eryl tackled a slice of rich chocolate cake with a sense of abandon. When she had almost finished she smiled happily at Nerys and said, 'That was brilliant!'

Then she looked across the room, the smile instantly leaving her face. Lewis was there, also eating cake as if nothing else in the world mattered. And with him, smiling at him intimately as she talked, was the woman who had given them both a lift from Pandy. The woman whom Lewis had introduced as Jennifer Vaughan.

Following her gaze, Nerys also saw Lewis. 'Well I'm blowed!' she said. 'So this is where he gets to. Want to go over and tell him off? About the mix-up over his patients?'

Eryl hurriedly drained her coffee cup and said, 'No. He's far too busy. So let's just go, shall we?'

'Is something wrong?' Nerys asked.

She was aware of the young nurse giving her a strange look but couldn't rid herself of the jealousy she knew must be showing on her face. Feeling stifled by it, she took money from her purse, slapped it on the table and said hoarsely, 'You pay, will you? I've just got to find a ladies' room. See you outside. With the cat food, if you can manage it.'

Fortunately Nerys just gave her a wry grin and said, 'Thank heavens coffee doesn't have the same effect on me.'

As she hastily left the table Eryl saw Lewis glance at her and saw surprise moving over his face. And when he stood up, looking as if he had every intention of joining her, she fled blindly in the direction of the powder room. Rushing inside and finding it empty, she went to the washbasins and sluiced her face with cold water. Taking a paper towel, she dabbed at her skin and leaned against a wall as she fought to steady her breath.

She knew that she was being utterly ridiculous. Lewis had every right to be with that woman. With any woman, come to that. Whatever he chose to do with his private life had nothing to do with her. She'd accepted that long ago, hadn't she? So why, in the name of heaven, was she suddenly feeling so lost?

Thankful that the powder room remained empty, she drew in a shuddering breath and allowed herself a moment of weakness by admitting the truth. She was feeling lost because she was jealous, damn it! And she had absolutely no right to feel that way.

Now she felt her blood draining away from her face and she was hurting inside. And she just didn't know what to do about it.

Squeezing her hands into fists, she pressed them against her forehead and closed her eyes tightly as she tried to stem the tears that were rising in her. At last she succeeded and, looking at herself in a mirror, she frowned at her ravaged face and took a compact from her shoulder bag.

Carefully she smoothed powder over the dark shadows that had appeared under her eyes and then pressed her pale lips together until they showed a touch of colour. Satisfied that she now looked more or less normal, she straightened her shoulders and walked towards the door but before she could open it Nerys came in, carrying the bag of cat food.

'Are you OK?' she asked. 'I wondered what had happened to you.'

'Just a touch of gippy tummy,' Eryl lied. 'Shouldn't have eaten that cake so fast. But I'm fine now so let's go, shall we? By the way, has Lewis left?'

'Yes. Ages ago. He looked as if he wanted to speak to me but it seemed his lady friend was in a hurry. She dragged him out quicker than you could blink!'

CHAPTER ELEVEN

ERYL had forgotten how swiftly the weather could change so dramatically in Dynas. One Friday morning, soon after she and Nerys had visited Trefor in Swanton, she could feel a hint of frost and she noticed that the mountains were shrouded in mist. By late afternoon that mist became dense enough to worry about so when she took a call from Mountain Rescue she wasn't surprised. But what did puzzle her was the nature of that call.

Usually Mountain Rescue warned all doctors in the area to stand ready and then got in touch again by rota if they couldn't manage without them. This time, however, she was named specifically and asked to come quickly to Craigwen, a remote pass high in the mountains some miles from the Pughs' farm.

'OK! I'll be there pronto!' she said, then asked, 'Why me in particular?'

'Because the man we've got here seems to know you. He's in a really bad way. He was semi-conscious when we found him but with no injuries as far as we can see. He managed to say a few words, though, and we gathered he's a patient of yours. But he refuses to be helped by us. Says he needs to see you first.'

'What's his name?'

'He won't give it.'

'Has he lost his memory, then?'

'We don't think so. I'd say he's just obstinate!'

'Right! I'm on my way!'

There wasn't time to let Lewis know what was happening so she left a message at the desk and flew into action at once, driving with full headlights plus a powerful fog lamp towards the pass.

Gareth Pugh had now been discharged as fit from the Swanton hospital and Eryl feared that the mysterious patient who refused to give his name could be him. But what on earth had possessed him to walk to this particular mountain pass was beyond her comprehension. Yet the nearer she got to Craigwen the more doubtful she felt about this man's identity. Gareth was really Lewis's patient, wasn't he? So why ask for her?

She knew the way well and managed to avoid every hazard by instinct. Nevertheless, she thanked all the Celtic gods she could remember for eventually getting her there in one piece. The rescue team, consisting of three men she had never met before, saw her coming through the mist and flagged her down with their torches, one of them asking in Welsh if she was the doctor.

'Yes,' she said quickly, braking and getting out of the car.

'Thank heavens! The man refused every kind of help until he'd spoken to you.'

Eryl peered at the inert figure lying at their feet, his head propped by a blanket against a boulder and with two more covering him from neck to toe. Then she drew in a swift breath. The man who now seemed barely conscious was not Gareth Pugh but David Morland.

'Right! Just give me a moment,' Eryl said as she knelt at his side, moving the blanket slightly to take his wrist and feel for a pulse. 'How long has he been here?'

'Can't tell. We came across him by chance while we

were doing the automatic sweep we always carry out when the weather changes so suddenly. Inexperienced walkers often get stranded. Not used to reading the early signs.'

'But this man should have noticed them. He lives here!'

The recluse gave a kind of croak and Eryl asked the men to shine their torches directly at him. What she saw worried her. Morland's face was grey, his staring eyes dull and his hands a mottled blue. Although the blankets covering him were thick they were insufficient for he already seemed to be on the edge of hypothermia. If something wasn't done quickly he could become frostbitten at this high altitude.

What he needed was immediate warmth but she didn't dare rub any part of him showing dramatic temperature reduction. If she did she would only make matters worse, perhaps even damage the iced tissue until the only cure would be amputation. There was also the danger of bacterial infection.

'I take it you carry aluminium foil?' she asked.

'Of course. But this wretch fought against it.'

'Well, he won't now. It'll be more than his life's worth. So please get it while I try my best to put a little warmth into him.'

The men went into their Range Rover and Eryl lay down beside David Morland, moving her warm body close to his, putting her mouth to his face and blowing gently at him.

He stirred a little and she asked if he felt any pain anywhere.

'Stomach,' he said thickly. 'Aches.'

Most likely the suspected ulcer, Eryl thought, in her mind already making swift plans to get him into the nearest hospital. Then she felt an arm moving slowly to her waist and eventually circling it. 'That's good,' she murmured. 'Cling on to me if you can. Soon we'll be able to wrap some foil around you, trapping the warmth you're getting from me.'

But before the men could return something happened that she thought would shake her for the rest of her days. David Morland regained enough strength to whisper in her ear and she could scarcely believe what she was hearing.

'I've dreamt about this,' he murmured raggedly. 'Ever since I first saw you. That's—why I wanted you to—release me. Then you would be—free to—love me. . .'

As his voice trailed away she recalled what Lewis had said about the man and shuddered. Immediately afterwards a second extraordinary thing happened. One of the men called out that someone else was arriving and she peered through the fog to see Lewis jumping out of his car.

He weighed up the situation at once, taking some of the aluminium foil from the men ready to help them wrap it round David Morland's body. But it seemed that he hadn't weighed up the situation accurately for, kneeling down, he pushed Eryl brusquely aside and said, 'What the devil d'you think you're doing, woman?'

'Trying to get some warmth into the man, of course! What did you think I was doing?'

Lewis didn't reply—just looked at her with blank eyes, his mouth drawn into a thin, bitter line.

She stood up, leaving the rescue team to finish covering Morland before they carried him on a stretcher to the Range Rover. 'Will you take him to hospital or shall I call for an ambulance?' Eryl asked.

'We'll take him,' one of the men said. 'Which of you doctors will be meeting us there?'

She hesitated for a moment, then walked stiffly to her car. 'Dr Caswell,' she said.

'Where do you think you're going?' Lewis asked coldly.

'Home,' she said, lowering her voice so that the men couldn't hear her and Lewis behaving like two spiteful children. 'You seem to be managing very well here.'

'But, for God's sake, the man's your patient!'

'You should have thought of that before you pushed me away.'

'Come back here, Dr Thomas!'

She turned to stare at him in the emergency light that the team had left burning while they made Morland comfortable inside the Range Rover. His face was pale and lined with anger, his body rigid.

'I'm going home,' she repeated, not caring if she hurt him. She tried not to remember the sweetness that had been between them and got into her car, switching on the engine. Then she told him to go to whatever hospital he liked—when she really wanted to tell him to go to hell. At last she drove off, her lights blazing just as brightly as her temper.

Later that night she regretted her anger and wanted to go to Lewis's cottage to seek him out and shower him with apologies. But each time that she decided to go something held her back. The gentle image of him making love to her had vanished, replaced by jealousy of a woman called Jennifer Vaughan.

Oh, she knew their night of love-making had meant nothing more to him than a physical coupling and she had accepted that. But the attention he seemed to be giving Jennifer, together with the anger he'd shown over Morland, was just too much to bear. The next day she saw him briefly to ask how Morland was but again offered no apology for leaving abruptly.

'He's doing very well but no thanks to you,' Lewis said. 'He's in Pandy, by the way. And, don't worry, I managed to cover up your absence. Told the staff that you'd been called to another case.'

She knew that she ought to explain why she had been embracing David Morland—that if she hadn't given warmth to him as she did the story could have ended very differently. But, seeing a kind of scorn in his eyes, she walked away.

As day followed day and Eryl realised that she had gradually lost all contact with Lewis she became increasingly depressed. There were times when he disappeared from the scene altogether, rushing into his morning surgery and then afterwards hurrying out as if he didn't have a moment to spare. But one afternoon she saw him in the courtyard as he was unlocking his car and decided to speak at last.

Although it was now early September the frost had gone and the sun still held the lingering warmth of summer. As her shadow fell across him he looked up, asking what she wanted. His expression was grim, as if he couldn't bear to be this close to her, and she almost turned away. Then, seeing a trace of misery in his eyes, she said, 'What's wrong, Lewis?'

'You mean you don't know?'

'I wouldn't ask if I did, would I?' She knew that her voice was unnecessarily sharp but just couldn't control it. She felt a stupid prickle of tears behind her eyes so she turned away.

Immediately he put his hands on her shoulders, turning her towards him, and she felt a little flutter of hope in her breast. But when she looked up at him it died. The expression on his face was filled with scorn.

'Crocodile tears?' he asked coldly. 'What a pity they can't be real.'

For a moment she was speechless. Then she found her voice but, instead of it being strong as she hoped, it sounded lost—far away as if it were coming from some other mouth. 'You're being unfair, Lewis,' she said. 'Bigoted, just as you've always been. Just like you were when we first met and you admitted you could never trust women doctors.'

His mouth twisted into a smile of contempt. 'Just give me one reason for trusting them, will you? Or, better still, tell me why I should trust you after I saw you with that—that womaniser, Morland!'

'But I wasn't *with* him! I was trying to put some warmth into a man who could have died of cold.'

'And listening to his secret words by the look of it.'

She stayed silent for a long time, just looking at him as horror mounted in her. What kind of man was he if he could believe that? At last she said, 'Oh, Lewis! Lewis! What is happening to you? And to think that I once believed I could love you.'

She hadn't meant to say that. But there it was and now she could never take those words back. Rather than watch the dislike that she knew would darken his face she turned away and fled towards her flat. She heard him call her name and imagined that she heard a softening in the tone of his voice. But she didn't look back.

*   *   *

The next few days were so filled with activity that Eryl scarcely had time to think about her strained relationship with Lewis. One event that kept her fully occupied was the supervision of David Morland's removal from Pandy to the hospital in Swanton so that Mr Over, a duodenal specialist, could examine him now that he had recovered from the hypothermia that had threatened him.

One afternoon she received a call asking her to come to the hospital as soon as possible so, fearing the worst, she made this her priority, going straight to the specialist in charge.

'Are you going to operate?' she asked.

Mr Over gave her a hopeless look. 'No, Doctor. For the simple reason that the man's discharged himself.'

'*What*! But I don't understand. How could this happen?'

'It could and it has. Unhappily, the patient is legally within his rights. Given that he's sane, of course.'

Eryl suddenly felt drained. She knew that there was nothing either she or Mr Over could do. Apart from visiting the man in his caravan, of course, which she was determined to do as soon as possible.

'I'm sorry. For all the trouble the man's caused,' she said.

Mr Over shrugged, then smiled at her kindly. 'It's not your fault, Doctor, so please don't blame yourself.'

She left the hospital, intending to visit Morland in his caravan later that day. But here she met an obstacle for the moment she returned to Dynas Glynis Jones told her that Nerys had been looking for her. 'Urgently,' she said.

Eryl found the nurse in the treatment room,

surrounded by a motley crew of patients, all expecting to hear a special talk on contagious diseases that Eryl had promised them. Nerys was filling in as best she could with other material they had planned together but a woman from the village was protesting, telling the nurse in a loud voice that she had been expecting something entirely different.

'I'm so sorry,' Eryl said, fixing a bright smile on her face. 'It was my fault. I was held up. Just give me a moment to find my notes, will you?'

With that she hurried to her surgery, took a sheaf of papers from a drawer and rushed back to deliver what turned out to be a very necessary talk.

When she had finished there was just time to snatch a sandwich before evening surgery began and by the time she had seen even more patients than usual because Lewis seemed to have disappeared again she was too exhausted to do anything about David Morland. After that, each time she thought of visiting him she found some excuse not to go.

Then something happened which blotted the wretched man from her mind altogether.

This was the return of Trefor Dillon one Friday afternoon. She hadn't seen him when she visited Mr Over in Swanton because he had been moved to a special recovery home near the coast. Now, filled with health-giving sea breezes, he arrived in Dynas looking more like his old self with a twinkle in his eyes again that warmed Eryl's heart.

The next afternoon the staff in Reception arranged a 'welcome home' meeting in his surgery, covering his desk with cards, plates of sandwiches and a huge pile of Welshcakes made with the tender loving care of Mrs Reynolds. There was also a good supply of soft drinks because Trefor wasn't allowed anything stronger while he was still on medication. Everyone was there, including old Martha herself.

'I'm here to keep an eye on my doctor,' she told Eryl, sounding as if she considered him to be her own personal property. Then she stood hovering over him until he waved her irritably away.

But Trefor didn't play fair. Instead of just enjoying this impromptu party, after Glynis and Betty had made speeches of welcome in Welsh and English he held up his hand and told them all that he was now going to change the gathering into a work meeting.

Lewis, who had joined the party at the last moment—avoiding all contact with Eryl—immediately put his foot down. 'You'll continue to leave everything to us. Including practice meetings,' he said firmly. Then added, 'Or else!'

'Or else what, my boy?' Trefor glared at his colleague with the light of battle in his blue Celtic eyes.

'Or else you'll become ill again.'

'That's rubbish! I never felt better. It's time I took over my share of patients.'

But Lewis persisted in arguing with him and just when Eryl thought that it was time to intervene before their scrapping turned from banter into serious bloodletting Trefor retired from a fight that he knew he couldn't win. Sitting down in the nearest chair, he went on glowering at Lewis and then his eyes suddenly began to twinkle with hidden laughter.

'Have it your own way, then!' he said, with no trace of malice. 'But I warn you. If you don't allow me to see a few patients in what, after all, is my own practice I shall fade away without trace.'

'But we won't allow that to happen, Dr Dillon,' Eryl

said. She then frowned at Lewis and added emphatically, '*Will we?*'

Lewis shrugged. 'If you say so.'

'I do. How about limiting his hours to a minimum to begin with? Vetting his patients so that he's presented with only the easiest cases? Then see how we go on from there.'

'Hey, young lady!' Trefor said. 'Just remember that I'm here, will you? Don't you dare to give me any of that "does he take sugar?" stuff!'

Although his words were sharp there was laughter in his face and the atmosphere immediately lightened. He moved around the room, chatting with everyone. Enquiring how Nerys felt and asking when the baby was due. Asking Eryl how the hygiene clinic was doing, then patting her shoulder affectionately after she had described everything in detail.

When he had spoken to everyone he began to tire so thanked them all and asked Mrs Reynolds to come back to the house with him.

Eryl insisted on helping to clear up. She was just about to join the others who were washing up in the treatment room when Lewis took a pile of plates from her, putting them down on a chair.

'You've done enough,' he said quietly. 'Why don't you go home and rest?'

This was the first time she'd been alone with him since their last disastrous meeting. Now she regarded him with suspicion, mistrusting the gentleness she heard in his voice. 'Why should I rest?' she asked coldly, turning away from him because she couldn't bear the warmth that suddenly came into his eyes.

'Please, Eryl. Don't be like this,' he said softly. 'Do you have to treat me like the enemy?'

She wanted to say that he'd got it all wrong—that he was the one who treated her as the enemy. Perversely she also wanted to lift her arms to him; to feel the warmth of him encompassing her like it had when, for a brief moment, they had become lovers. But he seemed to have forgotten the sweetness of that time and now she could find nothing to say that wouldn't end with argument.

He looked at her in silence for a while. Then he murmured, 'I owe you an explanation, don't I? I should have told you long ago that deep down I really believed what you told me about Morland. But, more than that, I should have let you know the reason why I kept disappearing from the surgery.'

She felt herself stiffen and, try as she might, could not prevent her voice sounding savage as she said, 'Surely there's no need to explain. I should have thought the scenario was simple. One doctor takes another doctor to bed. They make delicious love. He then leaves, swanning off while he expects the other doctor to pick up his patients—even though she's exhausted from her own workload.

'The next thing to happen is the first doctor's secret teatime rendezvous with a beautiful woman named Jennifer Vaughan. Explain that away if you can!'

He began to look grim and for a moment she felt fear running through her. 'What on earth are you talking about?' He was almost growling at her now, his eyes growing dark. 'Jennifer is an acquaintance. Nothing more. And as for swanning off, as you so rudely put it, I've been doing something on your behalf. Or, at least, with you in mind.'

She stared at him speechlessly. Was he slowly but

surely going mad? At last she managed to say, 'What is all this? Some sort of fantasy?'

'Of course not.'

'Then for God's sake tell me what you mean!'

'Not here, Eryl. Somewhere more private.'

The last thing she wanted was to be alone with him. That fatal charisma was beginning to eat into her again and she just didn't know how she would be able to control her responses.

'I can't stay,' she said. 'I have to go out. At once.'

His face paled as he stared at her bleakly. At last he said, 'You've met someone, haven't you? Some man with the power to make you forget the past.'

Let him think that if he wished to. It would make no difference. Now all she wanted was to escape. Yet she found that she couldn't lie to him. Whatever kind of deception he'd been practising on her, she didn't want to use the same kind of trickery with him.

At last thinking of a valid reason for leaving she said, 'Yes, I am going to see a man. But not in the way you mean. I'm going to visit a patient. David Morland, who's discharged himself from the hospital without warning.'

He frowned at her but she held her ground, staring straight at him. Then he said, 'I'm coming with you. And we'll go in my car.'

CHAPTER TWELVE

ERYL didn't relish another argument with Lewis so she collected her medical case from the flat and met him by his car. He drove towards the lonely place where Morland lived in complete silence and she was glad. She didn't think that she could cope with any kind of conversation at this moment. When they arrived she steeled herself to meet her difficult patient but as she stepped from the car and glanced at the hilltop she realised that something was missing.

'Where are we?' she asked, thinking that they had come to the wrong place.

Lewis, locking the car doors, didn't see the empty space that puzzled Eryl. 'In no man's land?' he suggested, with a faint smile.

'You could well be right. Look! There's nothing here. No caravan. No battered old BMW.'

Lewis followed her gaze and looked as puzzled as she did. 'Well, I'll be damned!' he said softly. 'The man's not only discharged himself from hospital, he's upped and left. Without a word.'

'Ought we to look for him? Suppose something terrible's happened?'

'If you think I'm going to tramp through these mountains without proper boots and a guide you must be mad. I would have thought you'd hesitate, too, after your last experience. Anyway, he's taken everything with him so he must know what he's doing.'

This sobered Eryl. 'Just the same, perhaps we should

tell the police to keep a lookout in case he's in trouble.'

'Right! I'll drive us straight there.'

As they went towards the car again a man appeared over the brow of a hillock. At first Eryl thought that it must be Morland but as he drew nearer she noticed two dogs at his side and saw that he carried a shepherd's crook. Then she heard the man whistle and watched the dogs bounding away, falling to their stomachs as the pitch changed. When another command was shouted in Welsh they bounded on again.

Eventually she saw them rounding up three stray sheep, driving them into a field to join the rest of the flock before the man shut a steel gate on them.

'What a wonderful display!' Lewis said. 'Good enough for sheepdog trials.'

She smiled. 'Didn't you recognise that man?'

'Not at this distance I didn't.'

'Dr Caswell, have you never thought of seeing an optician?'

He turned to look at her and then began to chuckle. 'That sounds like your remark about me making a good surgeon!'

'Oh, yes. That time,' she said, unable to keep her voice steady.

His laughter died and he said, 'It seems so long ago.'

'It was. But I'll never forget it,' she murmured.

She hadn't meant to say that. It had just come out. She saw him walking slowly towards her, looking strangely uncertain of himself. When Lewis half lifted his arms she wanted to throw herself into them and feel the comfort of their strength, the softness of his fingers, but she didn't move. As his hands dropped to his sides again she saw a terrible emptiness in him, making him seem so vulnerable that she could hardly bear to look at him.

'We'd best be getting on if we're to tell the police about Morland,' he said gruffly.

'I think we should wait while I ask that farmer you didn't recognise,' Eryl said. 'It was Llew Pugh, by the way. He'll know what's happened because the man's caravan was on their land.'

Llew greeted them like long-lost friends, telling them how his father was and thanking them for forcing the old man into hospital. 'He's as obstinate as the devil,' he said.

'And that's why he's still alive today,' Lewis said, 'so never try to stamp out that wonderful spirit, will you? It'll last him a few more years yet.' Then he asked if Llew had seen David Morland lately.

'He left a few days ago. Moved to Wiltshire because there's more magic in the earth there, he said.' Llew gave a chuckle that finally turned into a full-blooded laugh.

'He must think Wiltshire earth has special healing qualities,' Eryl murmured. And thought, who knows? There were many strange things that doctors didn't understand, for all their scientific knowledge. 'Let's hope he finds a cure.'

As they left Llew and went back to the car Lewis turned to look at her. He seemed to be aching inside, Eryl thought. Deep down where he kept his heart.

Suddenly he said, '*I* need a cure.'

The sharp edge so often in his voice was blurred and the softness of it touched her, stirring so many different emotions that she wanted to tell him to stop. But she couldn't because of the compassion that was swelling in her. Without thinking, she reached a hand towards him and felt the warmth of his fingers as they curled around hers. So gentle. Yet so strong and protective.

'Why do you want a cure?' she asked softly.

'You don't know? You can't read my symptoms, Doctor?' Eryl shook her head. 'Then let me tell you. I want medicine for an aching heart.'

She felt herself growing cold although the September air was still so warm. 'Because of your wife?' she asked.

His mood changed dramatically and he tore his hand from hers with a violence that frightened her.

'No! Not my wife! Not Marian!'

Lewis was shouting, his voice echoing all around the hillside. She imagined those echoes being really the spirits of the ancient Welsh, rising from Cader Idris itself—the place where legend said they were buried with their king. The illusion, which filled her partly with fear and partly with a wonderful sense of romance, was shattered when Lewis gripped her shoulders hard and shook her.

'Look at me, woman! Tell me what you see.'

'I see a man who is suffering,' she said softly, 'because he is still mourning for a wife he loved more than life itself.'

'You're wrong. It wasn't like that. So listen to me, will you? Then perhaps at last you'll begin to understand me.' He put one arm around her, drawing her close to his side. He began to walk with her straight up a path leading towards Cader Idris. Halfway along the track he guided her to a place where rushes grew and moss lined the floor of a little dell. Still facing the great mountain that dominated all the valleys beneath it, he pointed to its highest peak. 'Look!' he said. 'The sun will be setting soon. Watch the colours changing to all the shades of a rainbow and then tell me how you feel.'

She raised her head, looking into the far distance. 'The sky seems to be filled with magic,' she said.

'Just as life should be. As it could be if we would only let it.'

'You should have been a poet,' she said quietly.

'First a doctor, then a surgeon! Now a writer of lyrics who, according to you, seems to need the urgent help of an optician.' He turned to smile down at her yet there was still an aching sadness in him.

'You said you wanted me to listen to you,' Eryl said quietly. 'Is it about Marian? And is she the person you once said looked like me—that first day we met?'

He sighed. 'Yes. But you're really nothing like her. It's time you heard the truth. Only one other person knows what I've been carrying around in my head ever since she died and that's Trefor.'

'No one? Not even the woman you told me was only an acquaintance?'

'Jennifer Vaughan? Oh, she knows. Of course she does. She's a lawyer, who's been doing her best to sort out the horrific mess I found myself in soon after I came here.'

'I see,' Eryl said, not really seeing at all.

'Shall we sit here and watch the sky? Or is the ground too damp for you?'

She touched it, finding it almost tinder dry despite the rushes growing there. 'It's fine,' she said, sitting down and making herself comfortable beside him.

Then she listened, staring at the beauty of the changing light as he spoke to her about Marian. Revealing things that she found difficult to believe. Although they horrified her they at last made sense of all the darkness she had seen in him. And she felt her love for him growing stronger until it gradually overwhelmed her, as no other love had ever done before. Not even the depth of feeling she'd had for Robert was as strong as this.

Lewis told her that his wife hadn't been the only one to be killed in the car crash. Her unborn child had died too—along with the driver, who was also her lover. As he paused she remembered his reaction when Nerys had told them of her pregnancy and at last understood the bitterness she had seen in him.

A question began to burn in her. She knew that if she asked it she could hurt him even more but it just wouldn't stay hidden. So, taking both of his hands in hers, she said, 'Were you—the father of her child?'

He frowned, his face shadowed. 'No, I wasn't. She made that quite clear when she left. To start a new and wonderful life with her lover, she said. But the man she left with wasn't her first. I soon discovered there had been many more since she'd married me.' He looked at her, frowning as he said, 'Perhaps now you will understand one of my reasons for disliking women doctors. Why I've sometimes treated you harshly. Why I've often shown distrust.'

He stopped speaking, his face racked with a primitive pain that bit so deeply into her that she wanted to weep for him. She said, 'Why are you telling me all this? You don't have to torture yourself in this way.'

He looked at her solemnly. 'I'm telling you because it's only fair for you to know the worst about me. After all, you have to work with me.'

'But this isn't really about you, Lewis. You've done nothing to be ashamed of.'

'No? Then tell me why Marian was so faithless. Why

she never wanted to bear my child but was only too happy to bear her lover's.' He drew in a harsh breath and said, 'In my heart I've always known that I drove her to it. There's something in me that fails to give another person happiness. I seem to destroy things. That's why I never want to get involved again.'

She stayed silent, remembering how he'd pushed her from him the first time he'd kissed her. Now she wanted to tell him that he was wrong but didn't want to use clumsy words that could hurt him. Yet she knew that she must speak before he sank into the deepest misery.

At last she said, 'Whatever your wife did it was her own choice. She wasn't driven by you. People are never really driven, Lewis. What happens to them happens because of themselves.'

He gave a dry little laugh that was completely devoid of mirth. 'If you ever grow tired of being a doctor you'd make a damned good philosopher!' he said.

'Well, that's one more profession to add to our list,' she said, trying to speak lightly. 'So, how about another? When you were small did you ever see yourself as an engine driver?'

This time his laugh was filled with amusement and he caught at her hands, lifting them to his lips and kissing them so gently that it felt like the caress of a butterfly's wings. Then he looked at her over the top of them, his dark eyes glowing in the light of the setting sun.

'It will be autumn soon,' he said. 'The leaves will turn into gold and then disappear into the earth. Before that time comes do you think. . .?'

As he hesitated she said quietly, 'Go on. I'm still listening.'

'There's something I want to ask you. But I can't. Not yet.'

She was bewildered and had no idea what he meant. 'So, when do I get to hear this question?' she asked.

'When I've sorted out the horrendous mess my life's in at the moment. The legal tangle Jennifer Vaughan is trying to untie for me.'

'To do with Marian's death?'

He nodded. 'I thought everything would be simple because we'd both made wills, leaving everything to each other. But Marian destroyed hers so she died intestate. Then her lover's mother stepped in, saying that she held a document signed by Marian which left everything to her wretched son.'

'Has anyone seen it?'

'No. She said she'd mislaid it and instructed her solicitor to delay things until the paper is found.'

'Can she do that?'

'Oh, yes. Once there's doubt lawyers can be terribly cautious. Jennifer Vaughan is trying to force the woman to produce it or, failing that, persuade her man to give in.'

'Oh, Lewis. How terrible for you!'

'You sound as if you really care.'

'I do.'

'So, what—what are you really saying, Eryl?'

She looked at him, knowing that she couldn't keep it from him any longer. 'I'm saying that I love you, Lewis. You may not like what you're hearing. In fact, I know you won't. But it's the truth, all the same.'

He stood up, pulling her gently to her feet. 'But I do like what I'm hearing, Eryl,' he said softly. 'So *please* say it again.'

'I didn't mean to fall in love with you but I just

couldn't help it. If you want to send me away I'll understand. But, just remember, if your lawyer fails and you lose everything it just doesn't matter. The fight is only over material things, isn't it? What really matters is the spirit inside you. That must never be destroyed.'

'Come here,' he said softly, enclosing her in his arms, and she took comfort from his warmth, loving the way his fingers pressed into her back then moved to her neck, gently easing knots of tension gathered there. At that moment there was nothing sexual in his touch—just a wonderful sense of relaxation and the pleasure of being with someone she had at last learnt to understand.

'Why did you tell me you'd been doing something on my behalf?' she asked.

'When I was away from the surgery for so long?'

'Yes. I thought you were avoiding me.'

He looked appalled. 'Never! Oh, never that! I was trying to sort out all that legal muddle before. . .'

'Before what? I still don't understand how all this concerns me.'

He laughed softly. 'You don't? You really don't?' She shook her head, then almost melted in the warmth of his smile. 'My dear, sweet Eryl, it concerns you very much. I don't want anything from my past to spoil the present. But there's something else you should know. You see, I, too, have fallen in love. With you, Eryl. I just can't do without you. So, could you stand a long-term relationship with me? Perhaps even—marriage?'

She stared at him through the gathering shadows of twilight and a wild feeling of joy raced through her. Then it dipped down as she thought of her own past. After a while she said, 'But you don't really know anything about me, Lewis. I've always kept so much hidden from you.'

'I know all I need to know. For heaven's sake, you've just told me you love me, haven't you?'

'But that's not enough, Lewis. There's more.'

'You mean you still hanker after the man you were engaged to?' His voice was scarcely louder than a whisper and she saw a terrible bleakness in him.

'No, I don't still love him,' she said. 'But there are other things about me you should hear.'

'You don't have to tell me, you know.'

'I must. Otherwise all those old ghosts will haunt me.'

'Then I'll listen. Try to rid you of them.'

She saw such empathy in him that her hesitation vanished. 'When I'd qualified and was to begin training as a GP I spent a holiday here with my father. He introduced me to the surgery in Pandy so that I could widen my experience.'

She stopped, glancing at Lewis, and he said quietly, 'You don't have to go on if it hurts, you know.'

'But I must. I owe it to you.'

He sat down again, pulling her gently beside him. Taking her hands in his, he smoothed them with a delicate touch that somehow gave her the courage she needed.

'What Dada didn't know was the kind of experience he introduced me to. I met Dr Robert Davies, you see. A magic man, who had the power to make me do anything he wanted. I fell in love with him. Hopelessly.' She sighed as past pictures danced in front of her eyes, bringing a shiver to her skin. 'I was a virgin and he wanted me. But I resisted him because even then I wasn't sure of his love.'

She looked at Lewis and saw his eyes glowing with a sympathy that forced her to cling to her failing courage and at last she told him about the pain she'd hidden for so long. 'Robert was very clever,' she said. 'While I was still the virgin he craved he proposed marriage. Said it didn't matter us being together after that because we would soon be making everything legal.'

'So—you became lovers?'

'Oh, yes. For quite a while. But then I discovered his weakness for other women. I told myself it didn't matter because he always swore I was his only real love. And I—well, I just went on forgiving him. Over and over again.'

'So—how did it end?'

She tried to keep the old bitterness from rising in her. But she couldn't. It was there in her voice as she said, 'It ended when he found I was carrying his child.'

'Oh, my God! You poor, sweet angel!' He reached out for her, hugging her so closely that she could scarcely breathe. 'Did you—have an abortion?'

'No. And I never wanted one.'

'So you had the baby adopted?'

A little dry laugh escaped from her throat that was burning with tears. 'Not even that,' she said. 'It never even became a human being, poor little thing. I miscarried, you see. Quite early on so I never knew if I would have had a boy or a girl. I was told it happened because of all the stress. Maybe that was right. Or maybe motherhood was never meant for me.'

There! At last she'd told him everything. She stood up, unable to face him any longer, and walked blindly towards the place where they had left the car. She heard him coming after her but didn't stop. She wanted to give him space; wanted time to suspend itself so that she wouldn't hear him when he told her how disappointed he was because she was no better than his dead wife.

And then those hands that she loved so much were touching her again. Pulling her round to face him. And he was kissing her. With love. With frenzy. With every other emotion known to man. And she felt as if she were becoming a part of him.

He moved his lips away from hers and looked down at her with a smouldering warmth in his eyes. 'My darling! My sweet, poor, wonderful woman!' he said. 'Never walk away from me like that again. I need you. I want you. And I'll go on loving you until Cader Idris turns into dust.'

'That will never happen in our lifetimes. Not unless it becomes a volcano again.'

He laughed. 'Oh, you gorgeous, funny woman! Come here, will you? I need to taste the sweetness of your mouth again.'

She smiled at him with mischief in her eyes. 'I'm afraid you'll have to wait. There's something you seem to have forgotten.'

'And what's that?' He growled at her, trying to look like a bear, she thought. But failing because that magic smile was back again.

'Something terribly important,' she said.

'Oh?'

'Yes. Your favourite patient—and my favourite doctor. Had you forgotten Trefor Dillon? Don't you think he ought to be the first to know about us?'

'All in good time,' he said airily, his face full of laughter. 'First, a kiss.'

'Say "please",' she said, 'then I just might think about it.'

Afterwards she never could remember if he'd said 'please' or not. All she could remember was his warmth as he looked into her eyes and told her over and over again that he loved her.

MILLS & BOON®

Back by Popular Demand

BETTY NEELS

COLLECTOR'S EDITION

A collector's edition of favourite titles from one of the world's best-loved romance authors.

Mills & Boon are proud to bring back these sought after titles, now reissued in beautifully matching volumes and presented as one cherished collection.

Don't miss these unforgettable titles, coming next month:

Title #13 COBWEB MORNING
Title #14 HENRIETTA'S OWN CASTLE

Available wherever
Mills & Boon books are sold

GET 4 BOOKS
AND A MYSTERY GIFT

Return this coupon and we'll send you 4 Mills & Boon Medical Romance™ novels and a mystery gift absolutely FREE! We'll even pay the postage and packing for you.

We're making you this offer to introduce you to the benefits of Reader Service: FREE home delivery of brand-new Mills & Boon Medical Romance novels, at least a month before they are available in the shops, FREE gifts and a monthly Newsletter packed with information.

Accepting these FREE books and gift places you under no obligation to buy, you may cancel at any time, even after receiving just your free shipment. Simply complete the coupon below and send it to:

MILLS & BOON® READER SERVICE, FREEPOST, CROYDON, SURREY, CR9 3WZ.

No stamp needed

Yes, please send me 4 free Mills & Boon Medical Romance novels and a mystery gift. I understand that unless you hear from me, I will receive 4 superb new titles every month for just £2.10* each postage and packing free. I am under no obligation to purchase any books and I may cancel or suspend my subscription at any time, but the free books and gifts will be mine to keep in any case. (I am over 18 years of age)

M6JE

Ms/Mrs/Miss/Mr _____

Address _____

_____

_____ Postcode_____

MILLS & BOON®

Medical Romance™

Books for enjoyment this month...

THE REAL FANTASY	Caroline Anderson
A LOVING PARTNERSHIP	Jenny Bryant
FOR NOW, FOR ALWAYS	Josie Metcalfe
TAKING IT ALL	Sharon Kendrick

Treats in store!

Watch next month for these absorbing stories...

THE IDEAL CHOICE	Caroline Anderson
A SURGEON'S CARE	Lucy Clark
THE HEALING TOUCH	Rebecca Lang
MORE THAN SKIN-DEEP	Margaret O'Neill